HELLFIRE &
BRIMSTONE

Books by Angela Roquet

Lana Harvey, Reapers Inc.
Graveyard Shift
Pocket Full of Posies
For the Birds
Psychopomp
Death Wish
Ghost Market
Hellfire and Brimstone
Limbo City Lights (short story collection)
The Illustrated Guide to Limbo City

Blood Vice
Blood Vice
Blood and Thunder
Blood in the Water
Blood Dolls
Thicker Than Blood
Blood, Sweat, and Tears
Flesh and Blood
Out for Blood

Spero Heights
Blood Moon
Death at First Sight
The Midnight District

Haunted Properties: Magic and Mayhem Universe
How to Sell a Haunted House
Better Haunts and Graveyards

other titles
Crazy Ex-Ghoulfriend
Backwoods Armageddon

HELLFIRE & BRIMSTONE

LANA HARVEY, REAPERS INC.

BOOK SEVEN

ANGELA ROQUET

VIOLENT SIREN PRESS

HELLFIRE AND BRIMSTONE

Copyright © 2016 by Angela Roquet

www.angelaroquet.com

Cover Art by Rebecca Frank

Edited by Chelle Olson of Literally Addicted to Detail

ISBN: 978-1-951603-00-7

For the readers who have been with me and Lana from the very beginning. None of these books would have happened without you. I hope you all find what you're looking for, in this life and the next.

CHAPTER ONE

"Religion is what keeps the poor from murdering the rich."
—*Napoleon Bonaparte*

I should have known it was going to be a shitty day from the moment I stepped inside Reapers Inc. on Monday morning and saw a perky nephilim sitting behind Ellen's desk. The winged bimbo didn't notice me right away, as she was fixated on the electric pencil sharpener I'd purchased for Ellen's birthday last year. She turned the thing over in her hands and twisted her head from side to side, sending her red curls bobbing around her face. One index finger slid dangerously close to the business end of the sharpener. I hesitated before finally stumbling over my morality.

"Well, that's one way to get a free manicure."

She looked up with a start and slammed the sharpener down on the desk. "Hi—hello there. Welcome to Reapers Inc.," she said in a perfect infomercial voice. I hated her already.

"Where's Ellen?"

"Ellen?" She blinked, and her plastic smile stretched wider.

"The secretary you're temping for. You know, the actual owner of this desk and that pencil sharpener you were trying to maim yourself with." I raised an eyebrow expectantly.

"Oh? Oh! Yes," she said, her infomercial voice coming back with a vengeance. "Ellen Aries is no longer working the front desk. My name is Regina. I'm the new receptionist." Her wings fluttered softly and tucked behind her chair as she sat up straighter. The poor thing looked like she was waiting for a cookie.

I stared at her a moment, slack-jawed and speechless. Then I tilted my head toward Jenni's closed office door. "Is the boss in?"

"Do you have an appointment?" Regina asked. I snorted and headed for Jenni's door, taking long strides lest she decide to try and stop me. Ellen would have. Apparently, that wasn't in this one's job description. I barged in without further warning or obstacle.

Jenni looked up from her desk, her expression hardening as she read my body language, despite my baggy work robe. "I see you've met the new secretary."

"You're joking, right?" I pointed out through the open door, not caring that the twit sitting at Ellen's desk could see and hear me. "Ellen has been at this for nearly a *thousand* years. What grounds did you have for firing her?"

Jenni exhaled through her nose and scowled at me. "I didn't fire Ellen. She was reassigned."

"Reassigned to what?" I snapped.

"Low-risk, freelance harvesting." Jenni stood and walked across the room to close her office door, leaving Regina to pout at Ellen's desk without an audience. "You forget that Ellen worked for *Grim* for those thousand years," she continued in a lower voice. "The council was growing nervous about that fact, especially considering the clearance level that comes with the receptionist position."

I groaned and rolled my eyes up to the ceiling. "Bullshit. You never liked Ellen. Did you really think you could pass this *reassignment* off as simple politics, with *me* of all people?"

Jenni sat down behind her desk and adjusted the collar of her white dress shirt before folding her hands under her chin. She managed to look smug *and* annoyed with me, all at the same time. The expression was eerily familiar. I'd conjured the same one from Grim more times than I could count.

"We're also short on reapers," she said, her mild tone lacking the aggression that Grim often met me with. "The council hasn't approved a new generation yet, so we have to make do with what we have. Ellen isn't living up to her full potential."

I scoffed and grasped my hip through my robe. I didn't wear the garment for Special Ops assignments, but the new unit I had been put in charge of was quickly becoming a joke. Kevin and I had been collecting random, oddball harvests for months now, so at least the short-staffed excuse was more believable than the notion that Ellen was untrustworthy.

Jenni held her hands out. "If you're so concerned about Ellen, then you can have the honor of shadowing her through her probationary week."

"What?" I squeaked. "I have an apprentice. You can't dump another one on me. Isn't there some kind of rule against that?"

Jenni let out a haggard sigh. "*Probationary* week," she repeated. "Ellen doesn't need a mentor to play apprentice to. She had her initial training under Grim, remember?"

"Yeah, like, a thousand years ago." I made a face. "Besides, what if a Special Ops assignment comes up? Shouldn't someone with a more reliable schedule shadow her?"

Jenni's next sigh was less annoyed and more pitying. "We haven't had a new lead in months, Lana. The remaining rebel cells have dispersed as far as the council is concerned, and the Fates don't even request updates anymore about their missing souls. They've come to grips with their losses, and it's time we do, too."

Heat filled my cheeks, but I kept eye contact with her. "So that's it, then? The war's over, and now everyone wants me to just sink back to my rightful place at the bottom of the barrel?"

Jenni looked pained. It was no big secret that the CEO position could have easily been mine if I'd really wanted it. I'd pushed for Jenni to take the helm, and it was too late to retract my endorsement now. Not that I'd want to. Just thinking about all the paperwork gave me a headache—but that didn't mean I was willing to settle for pocket-change harvests.

I could see the wheels turning in Jenni's mind as she tried to find a way to smooth things over. "I'll arrange a nice bonus for shadowing Ellen," she said, fingering a stack of papers on her desk. Her brow furrowed, and she looked down, choosing to focus on some random file other than my scowl. "You should consider reapplying for the Posy Unit soon. Asha Dipika is eager to transfer back to the Mother Goose Unit, and it might be the only opening for some time. The best I can do for you beyond that is medium-risk harvesting. You don't have enough credits at the academy for high-risk work."

My shoulders slumped. I didn't know what I had expected. She was right, of course. There was no need for the Special Ops Unit, but it didn't make hearing it out loud any less discouraging. Sure, Grim and Seth were both missing. But they hadn't been spotted in Eternity for nearly a year. Not since the last Oracle Ball. And then there were the missing factory souls that everyone besides me was ready to give up on. But without a lead, there wasn't much I could do, short of wandering both sides of the grave with my thumb up my ass.

Jenni mistook my silence for consent. "I'll have Regina merge your workload with Ellen's." She pressed the intercom button on her desk phone, and I heard Regina's yip of surprise through the office door, followed by hurried footsteps.

"Yes, President Fang?" she answered breathlessly through the speaker.

Jenni frowned, but her tone remained neutral. "I don't suppose I have to repeat that, do I?"

"No, President Fang. I'll just... I'll... merge schedules?"

"Yes," Jenni said, biting off the word with heat.

Regina giggled nervously. "How do I do that again?"

I smirked before turning my back on Jenni and heading for the door. "Oh, yes. I can definitely see how this *reassignment* is going to increase productivity." I twisted around to give her a mocking thumbs up before showing myself out.

Back in the lobby, Regina was a flustered mess, surrounded by open manuals and disarrayed schedules. She gave me a pathetic look as I drummed my fingers on Ellen's desk.

"One more minute," she pleaded. "I-I know I can get this right."

I opened my hand. "Give them to me. I'll sort it out on my own."

She made a dejected face, but it wasn't very convincing. I could tell she was more relieved than anything. I didn't care. I just needed to get out of there before I took the damn pencil sharpener to her myself.

CHAPTER TWO

*"Everything is possible, from angels to demons
to economists and politicians."*
—*Paulo Coelho*

Limbo City wore autumn like a fine dress. Buckets and window boxes full of bright chrysanthemums were spaced down every sidewalk. Some were adorned with glittery ribbons or white string lights that reflected off the store windows and gave the city a romantic aura.

A nephilim street vendor outside the Phantom Café was selling paper cups of roasted nuts and pumpkin seeds when Ellen and I arrived. The sweet, warm scent mingled deliciously with the smell of freshly brewed coffee as the café's front door swung open. There was a line inside, so I made a quick detour for the nut cart. Ellen reluctantly joined me.

"How can you stand these things?" she whined, tugging at the collar of her new robe. "They itch something awful."

"Get a good fabric softener," I said over my shoulder as I paid the vendor and took a salt-crusted cup from him. I popped an almond into my mouth and offered the cup to Ellen as we entered the café and took our place in line.

She shook her head and put a hand over her stomach. "I'm too nervous to eat. I haven't been on the mortal side in centuries, and I nearly flunked my L&L exam before that." The L&L, or latitude and longitude exam, tested a reaper's familiarity with human realm to prepare them for coin travel. A passing grade was mandatory.

Ellen's face crumpled, dragging down the corners of her crimson-polished pout. "Jenni can't really expect that I'll have the hang of this in a week's time. Can she?"

I stuffed a handful of nuts into my mouth to avoid having to give a legit answer and made a noncommittal noise, adding half a shrug for good measure. I continued my nervous munching as we were directed to a table, and a waiter rushed over to take our orders.

"A skinny mocha latte," Ellen said in her honey-sweet secretary voice. So much nicer than the newbie imposter's.

I held up two fingers to let the waiter know I'd take the same, rather than telling him so with my mouth full. He hurried off to fill our order, prompting Ellen to switch back to her whining tone.

"I want my desk back. Do you think Jenni will change her mind if that birdbrain doesn't work out?"

I shrugged again, feeling too dejected by my own demotion to offer Ellen any hope. Changing the subject was the best I could do. "Are you coming to the poker game tomorrow night?"

Ellen's nose crinkled. "Is it going to be on the ship again?"

"Yup. Unless you want to play hostess."

"You know I can't." She pushed out her bottom lip. "Duster doesn't do well with company. It would probably cause him to ignite prematurely."

"Only if it means taking out one of your guests," I said with a smirk. Ellen's toy phoenix had a vicious disposition. He adored Ellen, but everyone else could rot in hell, and he took it as his personal responsibility to expedite that fate.

Our coffee arrived before Ellen could launch a defense on the bird's behalf, and I took the opportunity to change the subject again. Distraction tactics were my specialty lately.

"Do you want to hit up Athena's after work? Maybe we could find you a nice turtleneck to wear under your robe to help with the itching."

Ellen let out a heavy sigh. "I guess." She sipped her latte, gazing dolefully over my shoulder, and then her expression shifted suddenly with surprise. "Don't look," she hissed under her breath as I turned to see what had caught her attention. I froze and sat rigid in my seat, waiting for her to explain.

"Good morning." Maalik's rich, brooding voice rose above the din of the café. I felt my face warm as I glanced over my shoulder, spying the angel as he slid into the booth behind me.

"Morning," I echoed back, instantly regretting that I'd acknowledged him at all.

We hadn't said much more to each other than civil nothings since my hearing with the Afterlife Council last spring, when he'd let me walk into a room set for my execution. Strings had been pulled at the last minute to pardon me, but not by him. His priorities were more focused on following rules—rules I liked to bend too often for his taste. That discrepancy had more than a little to do with the death of our working relationship, not to mention our romantic one.

Ridwan, Maalik's brother angel and another member of the Afterlife Council, slid into the seat opposite Maalik. His eyes smoldered as they landed on me, and his face twisted with rage before struggling to feign indifference.

"Two cups of black coffee," he ordered for the both of them when a waiter stopped at their table.

A sad smile tugged up one side of my mouth before I could resist. "No zombie chocolate lattes these days, huh?"

Maalik mirrored my smile with a small one of his own, but he didn't say anything else before turning around in his seat to face Ridwan, his silvery wings fluttering softly as they settled against the back of the booth. I turned around too, giving Ellen a look that couldn't be mistaken for anything other than *let's get the hell out of here. Now.*

As we headed down Eternity Avenue toward the travel booth on the corner, Ellen sucked more enthusiastically at her latte, her eyes gleaming with hunger. Gossip always improved her mood. Unfortunately, it didn't have the same effect on me.

"What?" I finally snapped as we stepped inside the travel booth, unable to take her eyeballing any longer.

"I didn't say anything." Ellen grinned innocently before taking another long drink from her to-go cup. "But if I had, it would be to comment on how nicely the Keeper of Hellfire's wing has healed up, after he risked his life to help you take down the ghost market—"

"I didn't ask for his help," I said through clenched teeth. "He took over the assignment."

I left off the part about how Bub had saved my life in the end, while Maalik was incapacitated. The Afterlife Council didn't trust the Lord of the Flies, even after his name had been cleared, and he'd been barred from helping with the assignment. Not that that had stopped him from tagging along in the shadows.

Retirement had placed way too much free time on Bub's hands. I was reminded every time I spotted one of his tiny foot soldier flies following me around. The spying would have rubbed me wrong if I wasn't so certain it was to aid rather than condemn me, though the thought that one of those buggy spies might be reporting my encounter with Maalik was enough to fill my face with heat.

"You okay, sweetie?" Ellen touched my shoulder. "Doesn't look like your latte went down too well. I told you not to chug it."

"I'm fine," I said, giving her a forced smile.

We stepped out of the booth near the harbor and I paused to bump fists with Abe, the nephilim guarding the entrance, before continuing down the pier toward my ship. Ellen pressed herself in close behind my right shoulder, her eyes nervously darting around as she tried to stay out of everyone's way. Reapers scrambled across the docks, meeting up with their units or sailing partners to coordinate schedules. They maneuvered around a parade of lesser deities lugging merchandise toward the market area along the eastern coast of Limbo.

"Watch it," a feisty pixie yelped as he nearly brained Ellen with a basket of crystals.

"Sorry!" She ducked, and then stumbled forward as she stepped on the inside hem of her robe. I grabbed her arm just shy of her face-planting on the dock and pulled her upright.

"Keep your eyes open," I said, minding my tone. She looked shaken enough.

Her chin trembled and she tucked in closer to me, stepping on my heels twice before we finally reached the ship.

"I hate the docks," Ellen said as we stepped off the ramp onto the main deck. "I hate this robe. I hate the sea. I *really* hate the sea," she repeated, gripping the deck railing as the morning tide rocked the ship against the dock. In the distance, a horn announced the beginning of the workday at the Three Fates Factory.

Saul bayed out a happy greeting as he clambered up the ramp behind us. Kevin's helljacks joined in as they followed him aboard, and then Coreen finished their song with an annoyed woof under her breath, as if reprimanding them.

Kevin was a step behind, a donut in one hand and a coffee cup stamped with Nessa's shop logo in his other. I'd spotted him a coin for the morning treat in exchange for him taking my hounds along for his morning run around the city with the helljacks.

His eyebrows shot up when he noticed Ellen. He swallowed hard and licked his lips before turning a questioning look to me. "What'd I miss?"

I gave him a pained grimace. "Jenni decided Ellen should take up reaping, and I get to show her the ropes."

He looked confused, but he nodded anyway. "Anyone exciting die recently?"

I dug his docket out of my pocket and handed it over. "We're on separate runs for most of the morning, but before lunch we'll meet up at a hospital in Nebraska to collect a few strays from a Posy Unit fire harvest, plus one extra from your list."

Kevin perked at that. "Can I stop at the original scene of the fire and have the helljacks catch a whiff? I'd like to test their tracking ability on the job."

"Sure, but I'm leaving the hellhounds behind. I can't afford the extra coin on the days they're not really needed." The confession made me cringe, but it was the truth.

Now that I was living in Tartarus with Bub, the daily commute was killing me. I was making just enough to cover that, the ship's docking fee, and groceries. I was considering cutting the retirement plan Jenni had set me up with a while back. It was either that or crack open my stagnant savings account soon.

Saul nudged his muzzle against my leg, and I scratched his ears with a sigh, feeling sorry that I couldn't bring him along. "*Manto*," I said, pointing toward the captain's cabin facing center deck.

I'd given up the swankier cabin that consumed the stern of the ship. Kevin hadn't been interested in tagging along to Hell with me when we broke our lease at Holly House. He'd checked out several different apartments around Limbo, but when our paychecks shrank, he began sleeping on the ship. It didn't get much cheaper than that.

In my guilt, I'd offered to trade cabins with him. I was living in a mansion, even if it was surrounded by a smoking hellscape. I could live without the fancier ship cabin if it meant making my apprentice more comfortable with our sad pay grade.

Kevin didn't seem to mind the new arrangement. He'd been doing more work to the ship lately, and I'd even agreed to move everything over from our storage unit and give him the extra coin after our contract expired. He was using it to buy tools and building supplies for his remodeling projects. It kept him busy and out of trouble, and the ship had never looked better.

"I'll see you on the flip side," Kevin said, giving Ellen and me a casual salute as he headed down the ramp with his docket and the helljacks. Coreen watched her babies go and then headed for my cabin, pausing in front of me for a quick pet. She sneezed and gave me an accusatory look before continuing on her way.

Ellen leaned into me, but she waited for Kevin to disappear before voicing her concerns. "I can coin off with you, right? I don't have to learn all the coordinates today, do I?"

I puffed up my cheeks and blew out a troubled breath. "I think it's going to take more than a week to get you settled. Jenni better not have been pulling my scythe about that bonus."

The dock had mostly cleared off by the time we stepped off the ship. A few reapers vanished from sight as they rolled their coins, off to collect the recently departed. Ellen looked relieved to have the extra breathing room, until it came time for us to leave.

"You know how this works, don't you?" I asked. She gripped my shoulder and put a hand over her chest, closing her eyes tightly as if in pain. I cleared my throat and waited for her to look up at me. "I do this every day, all day. You're not going to die. I promise."

She blinked stiffly and took a deep breath. Once her nails retracted from my shoulder, I rolled my coin three times, sending us on our way.

CHAPTER THREE

"Don't take life too seriously. You'll never get out of it alive."
—*Elbert Hubbard*

Ellen's first harvest was a funeral, the easiest of low-risk assignments. They used to be my favorite. Sometimes, if my schedule was mild enough, I'd hang out and let the soul watch their loved ones gather around them one last time. It gave them a greater sense of closure and, occasionally, it gave them a good laugh. The stories they told were to die for—often quite literally.

"What if she's already left her body?" Ellen whispered, gazing down into the open casket of her first catch of the day, an elderly woman named Bertha. The old gal was surprisingly small. Nothing at all what I expected a *Bertha* to look like.

"Only one way to find out," I said, shifting impatiently from foot to foot.

A mature crowd was slowly shuffling toward us from the funeral home entrance, and I wondered how many of them I'd see again in the near future. The organist began to play a melancholy tune as everyone took their seats. Soft sobs and whispers escalated until I couldn't make out what anyone was saying over the collective chaos of grief, and Ellen continued to drag her feet.

"What if she's possessed by a demon? Didn't that happen to you once? I don't want to be set on fire." She twisted her hands together over her stomach.

"That was an accident. You'll be fine," I snapped, hoping she'd forgotten that that demon had been Bub. It *had* been an accident, and he'd had all the proper paperwork to prove his possession was legal. The soul wasn't even on my docket. Anyway, it was ancient history. And Ellen was only bringing it up to stall.

"This is really nice. What do you think it is? Walnut maybe?" she said, running her hands across the glossy lip of the casket. "If I were a soul, I don't think I'd mind staying in here—"

"Ellen!" I gave her a wide-eyed glare.

"Fine." She huffed and turned her face away as she plunged her hand through Bertha's chest. Then she ripped the soul out like she was a stage magician yanking a tablecloth— or rather, an amateur magician with a bad habit of ruining perfectly good dinner settings. Bertha didn't appreciate the reeling any more than I imagined fine china enjoyed being smashed against a wall.

"Christ Almighty!" she wailed, giving Ellen a horrified sneer. "If my heart hadn't given out yet, I'm sure that ride would have done the trick."

"Sorry," Ellen mumbled, her cheeks flushing. The soul straightened her Sunday dress and then jumped when she noticed me standing behind her.

"I'm dead enough. I don't need you spooks trying to rile me up," she barked.

I ignored her and turned to Ellen. "See? Piece of cake. Let's get her to the ship and try another one." Ellen reached for my shoulder, but I waved her off. "I *know* you know the coordinates for the harbor. I'll get you around the mortal side today, but you can at least practice coining off on your own when we head back to the ship."

Ellen let loose an exasperated sigh, but she didn't argue. Instead, she dug a coin out of her robe pocket and put her other hand on Bertha's shoulder. I waited for her to coin off before following.

After we'd stashed the soul on the ship, we headed out for two more funerals and a street racing accident. I was saving the more difficult harvests for after lunch, when Ellen would hopefully have her shit together. Failing to tackle the random odd jobs would look even worse than failing to find the rest of the missing factory souls, and there was one job on my docket in particular that concerned me.

The soul was a CNH, Currently Not Harvestable, from about a decade back. A sighting had been reported around the anniversary of its death last year, so theoretically it was expected to show again. If it didn't, it would have to be reported as CNH a second time, and the new report would bear my name rather than the reaper on the Lost Souls Unit who had let it get away the first time. Lucky me.

By the time Ellen and I made it to the hospital where we were supposed to meet Kevin, I was ready to start drinking the hard stuff. Ellen's method of extracting a soul had improved, but her whining had not. She glanced around the dreary morgue in the hospital's basement and made a disgusted face as her shoulders trembled.

"This place is icky," she whispered. "I think I prefer the funerals."

"Oh, it gets better." I snorted as she turned around and caught sight of the charred bodies laid out on a pair of autopsy tables.

"Ewww," she groaned, curling her fingers up under her chin. "Do I really have to touch... *that?*"

"Good grief, Ellen." I rolled my eyes and walked over to the first body. "It's for, like, half a second. Get over it." I reached past blistered, black flesh and gripped the spiritual matter beneath, pulling the soul free in one fluid motion.

From Ellen's docket, I knew it would be one of two teenagers who'd been caught unawares while playing video games in a burning apartment building. Not that I could tell them apart in their crunchy mortal state, but as souls, they were more distinct. I was able to match the first one up with the picture in his file—lanky build, scruffy blond hair, and the beginnings of a mustache that looked more like a pair of sickly caterpillars dangling from his upper lip.

"Anthony Richards?" I asked, just to be sure.

"Uh..." he answered, frozen in place. All except for his wide eyes that darted around the dank morgue.

"Great," I said, accepting his drooling as confirmation. I snapped the file shut and turned to Ellen. "Your turn." I cocked my head toward the remaining body.

Ellen made a gagging face and shuddered again, but when my eyes narrowed, she managed to take a tentative step toward the autopsy table. Her hand reached out, pausing inches shy of her charge.

"Ellen?" I said sharply.

She jerked her hand back and squeezed her hip with it before turning to glare at me. "I wouldn't be in this mess if you'd stayed out of Grim's business, you realize?"

"Ugh." I dragged my hands down my cheeks and groaned. "I was being blackmailed by Horus. You know that. *Everyone* knows that, thanks to the trash mags." I didn't have many secrets these days, which in theory should have made my life easier. *In theory.*

Ellen turned her nose up. "You should have gone to Grim when that happened. He would have put that deadbeat deity in his place."

"Grim tried to kill me the last time I saw him. Or have you forgotten?" I raised an eyebrow and folded my arms. "Look, if you don't want me to shadow you, I'm sure Jenni can find someone else—"

"Yeah, like that would be any better." Ellen huffed and her hand slid down to her side in defeat. She glanced over at the crusty body on the table and took a deep breath before attempting to touch it again.

The second soul was shorter than the first, though twice as wide. He tumbled out of his body and rolled off the table, but he recovered quickly, clapping his hands after he'd jumped to his feet, as if his spill had been intentional and for our entertainment. He looked like he'd been trying to grow facial hair, too—or else he was just too lazy to shave the splotchy bits of fuzz off his chin.

"*Ooh la la*," he said, following it up with a low whistle as his gaze rolled up and down Ellen. There was a hunger in his eyes I wasn't used to seeing in the freshly deceased. Human teenagers were an odd, unpredictable bunch, full of hormones and bad ideas.

"Daniel Marcum," I read from his file.

His eyes zipped across the room to meet mine and he bobbed his double chin. "Who's asking?"

"The Tooth Fairy," I answered dryly, taking in his over-crowded trap. "Looks like you've been holding out on me."

Daniel smirked and glanced up at his shell-shocked friend. "You like them mean, Tony. You can have that one."

I made a face at him. Then I grabbed both boys' shoulders and turned them toward the autopsy tables, eliciting a yelp of surprise from Tony.

"Aww, man!" Daniel was trying to play it cool. He slapped Tony on the back and cackled out a nervous laugh. "Well, you did say you wanted to get baked."

The soul files were pretty vague most of the time, especially when it came to low-risk harvests, but occasionally, pieces of the bigger puzzle slid together. I glanced through the boys' files again.

"You managed to *bake* six other souls in your building, too," I said.

Tony looked like he was going to be sick. "My sister was down the hall doing laundry. Did she make it out in time?"

I shrugged. "Don't know. She wasn't on our lists, but that doesn't mean someone else didn't harvest her this morning."

Daniel looked less pleased with himself. Tony wasn't interested in his jokes before, but now he was extra inattentive with the news that his sister might be dead, too. Daniel's accusing glare told me where he'd laid the blame. Seemed I was getting a lot of that lately.

I ignored him and glanced down at my watch. "Kevin's late."

"Only by five minutes," Ellen said.

"Let's go upstairs and check on him." I retrieved my coin from my robe pocket.

Hospitals put me on edge, especially after Bub's rebel ex, a succubus, had attacked us in one last year. She'd also attacked me in the parking garage of Holly House. It could have happened anywhere, so dreading these places didn't make good sense. I found the unwelcome anxiety annoying more than anything else. Fear was a lot of things, but rational was rarely one of them.

Ellen nudged the two souls closer to me and filled in behind them, a silent request to coin the whole gang upstairs, including her. We were really going to have to work on her transportation efforts. But I wasn't up for another fight today. I sighed and gave her a berating glare before rolling my coin.

Kevin's charge was supposed to be in the cancer ward on the fourth floor, so that's where I took us. The brightly lit hallways were busier up top. A festive bulletin board plastered with crayon-colored pumpkins announced an upcoming

Halloween party, and fake spider webs stretched from every available corner of the nurses' station.

Ellen gave the receptionist behind the wide counter a longing look, while Daniel gasped and dodged out of the way of a moving lunch cart. The nurse driving the cart sidestepped to maneuver around the front counter. Her shoulder brushed through Tony's. He remained in a daze and hardly seemed to notice, but Daniel's mouth formed an *O*, as if the idea that they were truly dead was still sinking in. Their charred remains clearly hadn't been enough evidence.

The chemical smell of disinfectant mingled with the bland aroma of hospital food—meatloaf and green beans. It was depressing. If I'd been on a mortal deathbed, there would be cake every single day.

Farther down the hallway, Kevin leaned against the open doorframe of a patient's room. His arms were folded casually across his chest, the watch on his wrist facing up as if he'd been scrutinizing it for some time. He spotted our lot as we approached and stood up straighter.

"The harvests must have gotten mixed up on my docket," he explained with a grimace. "I almost missed my last soul. They were getting ready to lower his casket when I got there."

I glanced behind him. "Where are the helljacks? I thought you wanted to test their sniffers."

Kevin's frown deepened. "I didn't want to waste any more time by going to the scene of the fire if *this* harvest file was off, too."

"Good call." I squeezed his shoulder and peeked into the room he was watching.

The soul we were waiting on, a ninety-year-old man named Theodore, sat upright on the hospital bed inside. A halo of gray hair encircled the top of his head, the spattering of sunspots making it look very much like an oversized egg smooshing a nest. The lunch tray suspended over his lap was mostly empty. He didn't look like he was struggling through his final breaths, but death was sneaky that way sometimes. Though to be fair, no one was ever *really* prepared for it.

A spoonful of orange gelatin paused halfway to the man's shriveled lips, and his cataracted eyes watered as they focused on me. "More dessert," he grumbled before slurping down another bite. "Cherry and lime."

My breath caught in my throat. Was he talking to *me*? That wasn't possible. Maybe he was senile or hallucinating. That happened often enough this close to the end, right? I turned back to Kevin and Ellen. Their surprised faces were all the confirmation I needed.

So much for dodging the council's shit list.

CHAPTER FOUR

*"The supreme art of war is to
subdue the enemy without fighting."*
—*Sun Tzu*

This could not be happening. I'd done everything I was supposed to. I'd yielded to the council and let them bully me into letting Naledi revoke my unsanctioned abilities. I couldn't see the potent auras of original believers anymore. That meant they weren't supposed to see me in their human form anymore either.

Didn't it?

I wasn't entirely convinced this soul could see me—but better safe than on the chopping block again. It was time to take control of the situation.

"These old-timers see all kinds of things on their deathbeds," I said to Kevin and Ellen. I forced a small laugh and shrugged as I moved out of the man's line of sight and further into the hallway. "Why don't you two head on back to the ship and drop these souls off? Then go grab a pizza and meet me at the harbor."

Kevin's brow wrinkled but he nodded slowly, turning to take one of the teen souls by the shoulder. Ellen didn't say anything as she laid a hand on the other boy, the one who had been ogling her since the morgue. He wrapped a meaty arm around her waist, but Ellen slapped his hand away from her hip, finally taking her eyes off me to glare at him.

I nodded goodbye as they coined off, too nervous to speak for fear the old man might hear and start demanding more dessert again.

Once I was alone in the hallway, I held my breath and peeked inside the man's room. He moaned softly as he shoveled jiggly, orange cubes into his mouth. Then he lifted the tray and slurped at the sticky residue left behind. He caught sight of me again when the tray lowered and beamed a big, gummy smile before realizing I'd returned empty-handed.

"Cherry and lime! Cherry and lime!" he cried and heaved the tray at me. It ricocheted off the open door and slid across the linoleum in the hall.

I stepped out of the way as a nurse hurried into the room. "What's gotten into you, Teddy?" she said, a hitch of alarm in her voice.

"Cherry and lime," he said softly, sobbing the words as he stared at me over the nurse's shoulder.

I swallowed and backed away from the threshold so that I was completely out of sight. The man was clearly a few headstones short of a graveyard. But there was no denying that he'd seen me. This was bad.

Panic blossomed uninvited, kick-starting my survival mode. Kevin wouldn't say anything. Of that, I was sure. Ellen was another story. Hopefully, she wasn't angry enough with me to report the details of this little incident to the council. It was highly unlikely that we'd encounter another original believer during her probationary period—as long as she didn't require more coddling than the week Jenni had suggested. But to be on the safe side, I made a mental list of the coin travel books I was going to have her check out from the academy library.

Once the damage control plan was in place, my heart slowed to a more normal rhythm. Then my mind tried to wrap around the bigger picture. Naledi *had* removed my ability to see a soul's aura. I'd tested that as soon as I'd come to after the procedure. It was a done deal. So why could this one see me? Was there something special about *him* maybe? I peered into the room again.

The nurse finger-combed Theodore's wiry hair, a tender gesture that failed to fashion the nest into anything even remotely respectable. "I'll be right back, Teddy," she said.

"Cherry and lime?"

"Yes, yes. Cherry and lime." She paused as she stepped into the hallway and bent to pick up the weaponized lunch tray before heading off to fetch more dessert.

I didn't want to go in the room and cause another bout of hysterics, so I paced the hallway, occasionally glancing down at my watch. I was going to have words with Jenni's new secretary. This timing mix-up had to be her fault.

The nurse returned a moment later with a heaping tray of *cherry and lime*, and I stole a quick glance into the room as she delivered it. Theodore—Teddy—overlooked my existence this time, having eyes only for his colorful desserts. I guessed it was one upside of a deteriorating mental state, how something so simple could bring such joy. A silver lining to his mortal condition.

I slipped out of the doorway as Teddy resumed his shovel and moan routine. A small headache was beginning to build at the base of my skull, and my stomach growled as I thought of the pizza waiting at the ship. It seemed callous, but I was so ready for this guy to hurry up and die.

Movement caught the corner of my vision, making me turn my head toward the end of the hallway. A set of double doors with glass windows marked the entrance of the cancer ward, and for a moment, I thought the woman staring back at me was merely a reflection, with her dark hair and wide, blue eyes. It wasn't until her face registered with alarm and she dipped out of sight that I realized my mistake.

Ruth.

I was running down the hallway before my better judgment had a chance to catch up. Ruth Summerdale was one of the missing souls from the Three Fates Factory. I'd harvested her in the 1920s, and I'd only seen her in passing a handful of times since then, on the streets of Limbo City. She'd always stopped to say hello and catch up, as if we were old friends.

There was no reason for her to run from me. But this thought didn't enter my mind until I'd pushed past the double doors and paced up and down the adjacent corridor, searching every room along the way.

Why had she fled?

And where had she gone? There was no sign of her.

I huffed in confused defeat and headed back toward my catch's room. This day was getting weirder by the minute.

As I reentered the cancer ward, I noted the absence of Teddy's audible feasting. His nurse was seated behind the receptionist area with the clunky desk phone pressed against one ear. A tissue was clutched in her opposite hand, and she sniffled as she swiped it under her nose and over her tear-streaked cheeks.

"His grandson was here this morning. Poor thing," she whispered to the person on the other end of the line. "I better let you go. Dr. Gregson is on his way to call the official time."

So, he was finally dead. My mood perked as I headed for Teddy's room. I was ready to be out of here and back on the ship. I stopped suddenly, realizing what a bad idea that was. What if he remembered being able to see me? What if he said something about it in front of Kevin and Ellen? I could always take him straight to Naledi in the throne realm.

Yeah, I thought, *because that wouldn't look suspicious at all.*

I was still trying to rationalize the best course of action when I reached the doorway of Teddy's room and froze. His soul stood beside the bed, wrapped in a hospital gown that gaped in the back and exposed his withered rump. He blinked down at his discarded body with wiser eyes than he'd died with. But that wasn't what had my heart bleating out an SOS.

A reaper stood behind him. One I hadn't seen in over a hundred years. One that I was certain had been dead for just as long.

"Vince?" It was barely a whisper, but all I could manage.

His head turned, dragging a long, black braid over his shoulder and down his back. Dark gray eyes twinkled at me.

My heart pinched, and I couldn't get my hands or feet to work.

A devious smile curled up one side of Vince's mouth as he gripped my harvest's shoulder. And then he was gone. Taking my soul with him.

CHAPTER FIVE

*"Reasoning with one who has abandoned reason
is like giving medicine to a dead man."*
—*Thomas Paine*

I'd never wanted to slap someone so badly in my life. Jenni didn't usually inspire that reaction from me. Sure, we'd had our moments. But for the most part, I felt as if I could trust her to do the right thing. And she knew me well enough to know that I wouldn't make shit up for the fun of it.

The most frustrating part was that I hadn't even shared the worst of my news yet.

"I know what I fucking saw," I said for the third time. More like, shouted for the third time. I stopped pacing her office to slap my hands down on her desk, slightly mangling her abundance of paperwork in my fevered rage.

Jenni cleared her throat and gave me a warning glare as she extracted a page from under my sweaty fingers. "I know what you *think* you saw, but it's not possible. Vince is dead. No one's seen him in well over a century. Why would he show up now? It doesn't make sense, Lana."

I rolled my eyes. "Then how do you explain the soul disappearing?"

Her brow furrowed skeptically as she turned away, and it felt like steam was coming out of my ears.

"I've *never* had to report a catch CNH," I said through clenched teeth.

Jenni's tone was more pity than malice. "And now you have two in one day."

I made a noise in the back of my throat, attempting to suppress my wrath. "That new secretary of yours screwed up the times on the dockets! Plus, that second soul was originally the Lost Souls Unit's fault. For all we know, it might not have even showed."

I folded my arms and flopped down on one of the benches in front of her desk. They were a vast improvement over the stiff guest chairs Grim had preferred, but they weren't very suitable for sulking in.

For a brief second, I considered telling her about Ruth—maybe even Naledi's botched procedure. But something told me that wouldn't help my cause. If Jenni didn't believe that I'd seen Vince, why would she believe anything else I had to say? She'd probably accuse me of grasping for straws, of making a desperate attempt to keep the Special Ops Unit active.

I couldn't help but wonder if she didn't *want* to believe me. She was pulling the wool over her own eyes, refusing to hear anything that didn't agree with her personal agenda. It was a Grim maneuver, and I couldn't understand why she thought it would serve her any better than it had served him.

Jenni avoided looking at me as she shuffled her paperwork into more tidy piles, leaving a wider section of empty desk up front, likely a precaution in case I had another out-burst.

"There were a few other scheduling errors today," she said, as if it was no big deal and to be expected of a new sec-retary. "The CNH reports will be expunged as soon as the Lost Souls Unit gathers the missing harvests—"

"Good luck getting that one back from Vince." I snorted.

Jenni stopped her shuffling to look up at me. "I don't want to hear his name pass your lips again. Do you under-stand?" Her eyes bore into mine. "My position with the council is finally beginning to solidify, and I can't have a bunch of bogus rumors shaking that fragile trust right now."

I was so frustrated, I felt like crying. I leaned forward, refusing to blink. She could play boss if she wanted, but this staring contest was mine. "And when they find out you've kept this information from them? How do you suppose that trust will fare then?"

A knock at the door made us both jump.

Maalik poked his head inside Jenni's office. "I apologize for the intrusion, but your secretary has gone home for the day." His eyes fell on me and he gave a curt nod. "Captain Harvey."

"Councilor." I nodded back, deciding not to correct him. I might still be a captain on the books, but I hadn't been one in the field for some time now.

Jenni stood up from her desk. "Please, come in." Her eyes darted to me with a threatening lilt. "We're done here."

It took all my strength not to storm from Jenni's office in a disgruntled huff. If not for Maalik's presence, I probably would have. I grumbled under my breath as I stabbed a finger at the elevator button in the lobby. As soon as I climbed inside an empty car, I impatiently punched the button for the ground floor.

I was so ready for this day to be over.

My stomach ached, and I remembered that I'd missed lunch. By the time I had made it back to the ship after the hospital incident, Kevin and Ellen were ready to begin the afternoon harvests. There was no time to waste, since the new secretary's timestamps couldn't be trusted. As made evident, yet again, by the second CNH soul I had to report that afternoon.

The only upside to losing ol' Teddy's soul was that I didn't have to worry about him outing me. Ellen was too frazzled over her training to bother asking about the strange outburst at the hospital, and Kevin was too busy making sure he didn't end up with any CNHs to add to our growing pile.

I saved my coin and walked the four blocks to the harbor rather than taking the travel booths. I needed to blow off some steam anyway, and the fall leaves soothed my sour mood. My heart felt lighter as I passed the city park, where the oldest and tallest trees canopied out over the hedge border that enclosed the quiet spot. I almost stopped to take a stroll through the memorial garden inside, but the hounds had been cooped up on the ship all day, so I continued on.

The lanterns were glowing against the fading daylight when I made it to the harbor. A soft mist stirred against the sea wall, coating the dock and making the boards slippery. Another nephilim had taken Abe's place at the entrance. This one didn't acknowledge me. It was just as well. I was too tired for pleasantries.

Most reaper ferries had returned for the evening, for which I was also thankful. Peace and quiet wouldn't fix anything, but it definitely didn't hurt. I hurried down the pier, shivering as a cool breeze lifted the hem of my robe and tugged at my hood.

Saul's bellow greeted me as I climbed the ramp to my ship, and he ran circles around me until I reached down to pet him.

"About time," Kevin said. He turned to finger the rigging knots. "Ellen went home—and thank goodness. She barfed up most of her pizza from lunch on our way to Heaven." He paused to smirk. "She was so green, Peter moved us up the line faster than he ever has. He was probably worried she'd retch all over the pearly gates."

I gave him a tired smile, too engrossed in the funk of the day to summon a laugh. "I guess it's a good thing we rescheduled our shopping trip for Wednesday."

Coreen skulked out of the center cabin and I patted my thigh to hurry her along. The helljacks trailed out after her, playing tug-of-war with one of Kevin's sweatshirts.

"Hey!" he hollered, chasing after them as they took off around the forecastle.

The distraction worked in my favor. I wasn't ready to answer the questions I was sure he had about the hospital.

"I'll see you in the morning," I called out before heading down the ramp. Coreen and Saul followed close behind.

When we reached the dock pier, I looked up at the ship and spied Kevin beyond the railing. The tight line of his mouth told me he knew why I was bailing so fast.

I waved goodbye as I rolled my coin. The hellhounds, recognizing the gesture, flanked me and bumped their shoulders against the backs of my thighs. Then I watched as the value marks faded along the rim of my coin and we were cast into the bowels of Hell.

Home sweet home.

CHAPTER SIX

"Religion is for people who are scared to go to hell.
Spirituality is for people who have already been there."
—*Bonnie Raitt*

Tartarus was a constant hundred degrees. I imagined the heat would be more welcome once winter took hold in the city. Like being snuggled in a warm blanket the second I arrived at Beelzebub's manor—at *our* manor. I was still getting used to the idea that this was my home, too. The hounds had less trouble with the concept.

As soon as we materialized on the much smaller dock at the estate's perimeter, Saul turned to nip one of Coreen's hind legs and then took off across the dusty plane that stretched between the house and the mountains in the distance. Coreen bounded after him, her tongue slipping happily from the side of her mouth. They loved the freedom out here, and their birthplace was a few miles south, where Hades and Persephone dwelled.

I smiled after my hounds, deciding to let them play until dinner, and then headed up the rock steps that led to the front entrance. It was a longer walk than before, the new house being situated farther away from the shore of the River Styx. The exterior lamps flickered on, lighting my way through the dusky pink hue of evening.

The original manor had been a combination of stone castle and log cabin, and while it had been beautiful, Bub had been eager to choose a different style and design. He'd waxed poetic about fresh starts and making the project a labor of love that included both of our visions, but I knew there was more to it than that. The number of enemies we'd both made in recent years inspired caution and a deep craving for security.

The exterior of the manor was innocently decorative, stone accents scattered across stucco, but beneath the façade loomed a fortress of steel beams and thick, concrete walls. The sea of windows reflecting the fiery sky were crisscrossed with a web of fine titanium cables, and if the security system's face-recognition software detected an unidentifiable guest approaching the property, retractable steel doors would slide out and seal the place up tighter than a nun's habit.

A black orb protruding from the ceiling of the porch made a soft noise as I finished my climb, and I heard the series of locks on the front door click open as I reached for the handle.

Inside, the air conditioning was working overtime. The stone and stucco design spilled into the foyer, and several giant pots of ornamental grass gave the space an outdoorsy feel. Only the glossy gray hardwood gave away the room's proximity to the rest of the house.

I stripped out of my work robe and kicked off my boots, stuffing everything in a closet off the foyer. Then I padded through the dark sitting room, a lonely space we'd mostly ignored since moving in, and entered the kitchen.

The floor plan was more open here, the dining area viewable over a semi-circular, marble counter that marked off the chef's arena. Another sitting area, one that we'd actually broken in, finished off the rear of the house. French doors laced with more titanium cables and frosted glass opened onto a wide patio, and a circular staircase in the corner led up to the master suite and bath. There was a small office, a parlor, and a guest bedroom on the main floor too, but the loft was for us.

I began up the stairs, ready to change into fresh clothes, but Bub's melodic voice changed my direction.

"My love, my dark temptress of the night," he called from the patio, beyond the open French doors. "Come see me."

I stepped outside, taking in the half acre of freshly tilled earth that was our backyard and Saul and Coreen beyond that, two black dots racing across the horizon. Bub stood in front of an open gas grill, a white apron fastened around his neck and waist. He prodded a steak with a barbecue fork and flipped it over.

"That smells good," I said, coming up on my toes to kiss his cheek. I ran my fingers through his hair and returned the grin he gave me.

"I've already pulled the kabobs," he said. "And there's a bowl of salad in the refrigerator. I hope you're hungry."

"Starving." My stomach flip-flopped in anticipation, and I was reminded of my awful day.

Bub's brow creased as my smile waned. "I noticed you skipped lunch," he admitted, not even the least bit ashamed of his snooping.

"Jenni has a new secretary who botched my schedule." I sighed and turned my gaze to the upturned desert. "The landscapers reschedule again?"

Bub grumbled under his breath before answering. "They'll be here tomorrow. I called the satyr who bid the job and told him that if his crew doesn't show this time, I'll be hiring someone else to complete the project."

The garden was the last piece of the puzzle. It was also one thing I had steered clear of. The only reason my thumb ever turned green was if I had it knuckle deep in a hellcat's eye socket. Besides, Bub needed something to keep him occupied now that he was essentially retired. Something other than spying on me, that is.

"I'm going to change before dinner," I said, leaning in for another kiss. He turned this time and caught my lips with his, moaning a sensual note deep in his throat.

"Hurry back. I missed you today." His bottom lip pouted out and I couldn't help but kiss him again. Maybe I wouldn't cancel that retirement plan just yet.

I slipped inside and took the stairs up to our bedroom two at a time. As I shimmied out of my jeans and sweater and into a pair of clean shorts and a lighter blouse, I noticed that the bed had been made. It wasn't the hotel pro job that Jack was known for, but I was impressed. If I had the kind of time to kill that Bub did, I was sure it would be spent binge watching John Wayne movies. *Or snacking*, I thought as my stomach growled again.

When I returned outside, Bub had the patio table set and our plates loaded with steak and roasted vegetables. He'd discarded the apron and looked rather edible in a pair of board shorts and a buttoned-down shirt with the sleeves rolled up to his elbows. We traded admiring glances as I filled a pair of wine glasses, and he fixed our salads. A chandelier of jar candles hung from the pergola overhead, glowing brightly against the darkening sky and pulling the romantic scene together nicely. It was pretty clear I'd be getting lucky tonight.

Saul and Coreen lapped from a metal water bowl at the other end of the patio. Matching bowls of Cerberus Chow waited for them. The steak bones would keep them busy for a while after dinner, giving us enough time to enjoy each other before our bed was invaded.

Bub pulled out my chair. "I want to hear all about your day," he said as I sat down. He scooted the chair forward, tucking my legs under the table, and then circled around to his side and sat down across from me.

I smirked and took a sip of my wine. "You mean you haven't already?"

He actually blushed this time. "I'll have you know that my foot soldiers don't follow you everywhere," he said, shaking out his napkin and folding it across his lap. "I never send them into the Reapers Inc. building—Holly would undoubtedly notice—and they don't even tag along to the mortal side most of the time."

"Most of the time?" I scoffed and raised an eyebrow. "I'm sure that's not for lack of trying."

Bub reached across the table to take my hand. "You know I'm just trying to be helpful. The rebels are lying low. They didn't *disappear*. I want to be there should they decide to rear their ugly heads again."

I nodded and rolled my eyes as I took another drink of wine. It was a tired conversation that we'd had enough times, and I wasn't so bothered by his protective detail that I felt like drudging through the whys of it again tonight. I was more interested in the bleeding steak on my plate.

"Is that a moo I hear?" I poked it with my fork.

Bub blinked down at his own plate and gasped softly. "Apologies, love. That one's mine." He swapped our meals and I gave the medium-done steak a more approving look before attacking it. Bub watched me, a teasing grin drawing up one side of his mouth.

"Save room for dessert," he said with a wink.

I returned his devilish look and stuffed another bite of steak into my mouth before having more wine. "You'll never believe who I saw today," I said, once my hunger had tapered off enough for me to pause and take a breath.

"Hmmm?" Bub said around a mouthful of salad as he looked up at me. The golden flecks in his eyes sparkled under the candlelight. It was hypnotizing, and I almost forgot what I was saying. "Who's that?" Bub asked, reminding me.

"Vince Hare, the reaper Grim supposedly terminated a hundred years ago."

Bub's fork clattered noisily to his plate. He swallowed hard before looking up again. "Where did you see this miscreant, exactly?"

"On the mortal side. During a harvest. He stole my catch." I wiped my napkin across my mouth and frowned at him. "Did *you* know he was alive?"

He sucked in a tense breath and ran his forked tongue over his teeth slowly, as if considering his next words. "Let's not ruin our lovely dinner with talk of such things—"

"Hey, you asked about my day." When he didn't reply, I set my fork down and folded my arms over the table. "I thought we agreed not to keep secrets anymore."

"We did." He nodded slowly, a deep furrow marring his brow.

"Then tell me, did you know he was alive?"

"I suspected, but there was never any proof. Azazel was the Hell Committee's representative on the Afterlife Council at the time, and the matter hadn't concerned him, ergo it didn't concern me."

A million questions came to mind and began rolling off my tongue. "Why would Grim lie about that? Wasn't he afraid it would come to light? Why not send someone after him?"

"He did." Bub pressed his lips together and gave me an apologetic frown. "Saul Avelo."

CHAPTER SEVEN

"We all feel the urge to condemn ourselves out of guilt, to blame others for our misfortunes and to fantasize about total disaster."
—Deepak Chopra

It didn't make sense. No matter how many times I tried to rationalize why Saul would have let Vince go, my mind refused to stop its endless racing. It spoiled the rest of the romantic evening Bub had so meticulously planned.

I nibbled through the remainder of our dinner, my appetite stunted by the depressing details I had demanded to know. Even the bubble bath I shared with Bub afterward was less stimulating, I was so distracted. When he slipped an arm around my waist after we'd climbed into bed, rather than trying to ravish me, I knew I'd blown my chance at seeing any action tonight. I sighed and squeezed his arm, a silent apology for my negligence.

Sleep didn't come easily. I lay awake in bed, listening to Bub's deep breaths as they danced across the back of my neck, and I remembered things that I had thought were long forgotten.

The past was painful. Bittersweet memories laced through with regrets and wishes.

After my hundred-year apprenticeship ended, I'd tried to stay in touch with my mentor. We'd become good friends and enjoyed catching up at the end of the day, when we transported our collected souls on to the afterlives. He'd continued to share the cargo hold of his barge with me for a few decades after our official pairing had concluded, until I'd saved up enough to purchase a small boat of my own.

Saul's territory had been England when I came along in 1709. As the years passed, we found ourselves being directed over to the British colonies in the New World more and more. We harvested medium-risk souls mostly, occasionally being pulled away to help reap casualties of the French and Indian Wars. The American Revolution that came later had been the highlight of my youth.

Industrialization and westward expansion had eventually split our paths. The New World was becoming a bigger place. A more violent place. The Mexican-American War, the Apache Wars, the American Civil War—it was a busy season for death merchants. The Franco-Mexican War took me farther south, and it also spurred my interest in learning French and adding a new European territory to my list. I had been an ambitious thing.

Saul's mood shifted when I began drawing more attention. I started seeing less and less of him. He spent longer hours on his harvests, enjoying the atmosphere of the Wild West and adopting the new look as his own, with his trademark cowboy hat. We were cordial enough whenever we ran into each other, but there was a tension that hadn't been there before. I couldn't put my finger on it.

It was a mystery I still hadn't solved when the news came of his death. I was devastated. Gabriel, too. The memorial statue was erected in the city park, and then life went on. At least, it did for everyone else. The depression I sank into quickly demoted me to low-risk harvesting and Grim's watch list. I stayed there for quite some time.

I couldn't help but wonder if the distance Saul had put between us was somehow related to his death or the sudden appearance of Vince, now that I knew the role Saul had played—or was supposed to have played—in the reaper's termination. Maybe I could ask Vince next time I ran into him. In say, oh I don't know, another hundred years. As long as he didn't coin off without so much as a hello again.

I tried to remember who Vince had been close to, his mentor or sailing partner. Maybe they would know something useful. Then my mind circled back to Ruth Summerdale. Her appearance couldn't have been a coincidence. Had Vince used her to distract me?

It doesn't make sense. The futile mantra plaguing my mind fired up again. I was in for a long, sleepless night.

CHAPTER EIGHT

"Peace cannot be achieved through violence,
it can only be attained through understanding."
—*Ralph Waldo Emerson*

Tuesday morning didn't start off any better than Monday had. I found Ellen's griping extra annoying without a full night's sleep, but my distracted mind filtered out her nasally whining, rendering it into white noise as we entered a funeral home to harvest a pair of souls. At least we didn't have to worry about timestamps being off on this particular job.

"Ellen," I said, interrupting her rant, something about the mothball smell of the oriental carpet. "Did you know that Saul was sent to take care of Vince Hare back in the day?"

She took a startled breath and blinked at me. "Who told you that?"

"Does it matter?" I cocked an eyebrow. "I'm just curious if you knew. I mean, you had to know, right? You were the secretary."

Ellen's face hardened at the past tense reference to her former job. "And as the secretary, I was sworn to keep the company's business dealings private."

We neared the casket display area, and I paused to swat away a fly as it buzzed past my face. "Saul's dead. Grim's MIA.

What's the harm in confirming something I already know?" The fly buzzed again, tickling my ear this time, and I wondered if it was of the mundane variety or one of Bub's. As he had confessed the night before, they didn't usually follow me to the mortal side.

Ellen sniffed and lifted her nose in the air. "Grim always favored Saul. He got the most attention during our training. Grace compensated by hitting the books, so I was left with the short straw, forced to take on the job with the most responsibility and the least reward." Her chin dropped, and she gave me a sad smile. "That's how it goes, isn't it? It took a long time for me to be okay with my humbler status. For centuries, I wanted nothing more than the respect my prestigious counterparts commanded. And now look at me. I'm a train wreck."

I sighed and squeezed her shoulder. "I'm sorry. If it were up to me, you'd be at your desk." I tried to give her a sympathetic face, hoping my eagerness wasn't bleeding through.

"Yes," she finally said. "I knew Saul was the one they sent after Vince. Who else would Grim trust to take care of such a task?"

I pressed my lips together and nodded before turning my attention back to the casket. I wasn't ready to tell her that Saul had failed, and Vince was alive. Jenni's warning about starting rumors didn't carry the same level of danger as a threat from Grim would have, but I didn't want to open that can again until I had more solid proof.

To thank Ellen for spilling, I extracted the soul on her docket as well as mine. They were set up in adjoining rooms that matched in every way, and I wondered how many drunk uncles had gotten lost on their way back from the restrooms.

As we were leaving the funeral home with our catches, Ellen paused and faced me again. She fingered her coin nervously. "It probably doesn't matter, like you said, but there's another detail you might find interesting about Vince's termination."

"What's that?" I asked, trying to maintain my false indifference.

"He wasn't selling souls on the ghost market like the papers all said."

"No?"

Ellen shook her head slowly. "He was stashing them somewhere on the mortal side. As far as I know, none were ever found."

"Huh," I said, trying not to sound too interested, and then rolled my coin as my heart hammered excitedly.

Vince was alive, and he was snatching up souls for some nefarious purpose. That was as good a reason as any to open a Special Ops investigation. Not that Jenni would approve it. And I was still left with the question of why Saul hadn't put an end to Vince's crimes when he'd been ordered to by Grim.

Had my mentor been part of this crime ring on the mortal side? Did the Wild West seduce him with romantic visions of life as an outlaw? The most pressing question of all though, and one that pulled my heartstrings taut, was whether or not Saul could be alive, too. Could he be hiding out on the mortal side along with Vince?

The day dragged on, despite my efforts to rush. I didn't push Ellen as hard as I probably should have, but I hoped she took it as a kind gesture rather than me being distracted. I just needed to be alone with all the turmoil spinning around inside my head.

After I dropped the last of my souls off at the ship and said goodbye to Ellen and Kevin, I headed into the city. I'd left the hounds in Tartarus for the day, saving a bit of coin, and decided to spend it on a hot apple cider that I took with me to the park.

The circle of tulip trees that surrounded the reaper memorial garden had yielded to autumn, rendering their leaves a rich, sunny yellow. The boughs were quite full, even though enough leaves had fallen to create a matching carpet of maize around the bronze statues of Saul and Coreen. I headed for Josie's memorial bench a few yards away, and then froze when I realized it was occupied.

Adrianna Bates was not a fan of mine. Of all the currently living reapers, she managed to squeeze the most guilt out of me. She didn't even have to say anything. It was the way she looked at me, her eyes cold and unblinking, as if she could see right through me and was not impressed.

I didn't have anything against Adrianna. She'd been Josie's mentor, so I'd heard plenty of epic tales that starred her in a shiny, favorable light. She had also been the captain of the Posy Unit before the job was turned over to me briefly. Now she was the captain of the Mother Goose Unit and dedicated to working with child souls. It was hard not to like her, even if she hated my guts.

I was considering whether I should leave when Adrianna glanced up and caught sight of me. Her neutral features hardened, and the line of her jaw went rigid. She tucked her long hair behind both ears and stood.

As she stalked past me, I couldn't help myself.

"I can come back later, if you want," I said, struggling to get the words out. I felt like I should have been apologizing for something. Anything.

Adrianna stopped suddenly and scoffed as if she couldn't believe I had the nerve to dare speak to her. I could tell she had something to get off her chest, and part of me wished she'd get it over with.

"You blame me, don't you?" I asked. Cider sloshed over the rim of my cup, and I realized my hands were shaking. "I didn't force Josie into anything. You were her mentor. You should know that better than anyone."

Adrianna's face flushed as she turned around to glare at me. Her fingers clenched and unclenched, as if she were desperately trying to refrain from strangling me. She finally stuffed them in the pockets of her jean jacket. "Maybe you didn't force Josie to tag along during your short-lived tour of the upper tier. I'll give you that much," she said, a bitter laugh punctuating her speech. "But you can't deny she'd be alive if she'd stayed clear of you."

Her words drew the breath right out of my lungs. I had no reply. Adrianna, sensing my despair, hurried on before I could collect myself.

"And Coreen, she was like a sister to me. But she met her end during one of your escapades too, didn't she?" Her eyes glossed over with tears, and I felt them well in my eyes at the same time.

Adrianna sniffled and glanced over her shoulder toward the memorial statues. Dusk was darkening the sky, and the light feature tucked inside Coreen's statue's lifted hand flickered to life, mimicking the final, valiant moment of her last battle. I'd been there to witness it. I wondered if Adrianna would have felt any differently about me if she'd been there too, to see that I'd been following Coreen's lead, not taking it.

"For all I know," Adrianna went on—because she obviously hadn't wounded me enough, "Saul might be alive too if you hadn't come along. Hell, if Grim hadn't made you his apprentice, we might even still be together." A tear slipped from the corner of one eye and ran down her cheek, and for once, I fully understood her hatred of me.

"You can't fault me for the things I had no control over," I said softly, wiping away my tears with the palm of one hand. "I didn't want any of this to happen to anyone."

Adrianna's features went cold again as she cleared her throat. "Doesn't matter. They're gone, and you're here. So, I'm going to take the advice I wish they all had and stay as far away from you as possible." She turned on her heels and stormed out of the garden, leaving me alone with what was left of those we'd both lost.

I sipped my cider, trying to calm my nerves. It was lukewarm now, and the sweetness was almost too much after the bad taste Adrianna had left in my mouth. A gentle wind kicked up the leaves on the ground, spinning them around the scattered benches under the tulip trees.

Saul's bronze statue seemed less jolly than I remembered. Blank eyes stared down at me as I approached. I wouldn't find any answers here. I knew that. But who else was I going to ask these questions? Even if Saul was alive, he clearly didn't want to talk to me. At least, he hadn't for the last hundred years.

"Did I know you at all?" I whispered to the replica of my late mentor.

A golden leaf floated down from above, landing on the wide brim of the Saul statue's hat where several others had gathered. In the evening light, it looked like a crown of thorns, and it inspired more answerless questions. Had Saul hung himself out to dry? Had his death really been at the hands of rebel demons in the line of duty? Or had he been mixed up in something more sinister with the likes of Vince Hare, the rogue reaper he had spared?

The church bells at Our Lady of Immaculate Reception rang out seven times, announcing the hour. I was late for the poker game on the ship. I tossed my spoiled cider in the trash bin on my way out of the park and headed toward the harbor.

CHAPTER NINE

*"I stayed up all night playing poker with tarot cards. I got a full
house and four people died."*
—*Stephen Wright*

Kevin had done an amazing job of renovating the ship. The
seldom-used rooms below deck, the ones that Josie and I had
been content to ignore, were really shaping up. The dining hall
off the kitchen was especially nice.

Vintage lanterns lit the space, reflecting off all the freshly
lacquered woodwork that spanned nearly every square inch of
the cabin. The row of windows that stretched down one side
of the room had been polished, and the hinges oiled, and the
broken mirror behind the bar had been replaced. Kevin had
also repaired one of the old tables and its matching set of
chairs. The rest of the worn or damaged furniture was piled
up in another room, waiting for a rainy day.

If not for the addition of a flat-screen, I was sure this was
exactly how the room must have looked in its prime, when
Grace O'Malley captained the ship. I envisioned her at the
bar, a slew of pirates crowding 'round, throwing back pints as
they hung on her every word. The history here was palpable,
and I loved it. I knew Josie would have, too.

While there were no pirates to speak of, the poker table was full tonight, with three sets of wings taking turns fluttering like claustrophobic pigeons in a birdbath. Gabriel's full-sized pair took up the most space, so Kevin and I had tried to balance the setting by taking the chairs on either side of him. Ross, the captain of the Nephilim Guard and Gabriel's roommate, sat on the other side of Kevin, and between Ross and me sat Abe, my favorite dock guard, completing our motley crew.

Gabriel shuffled the Death Deck as he eyeballed me. "Now that we're all here"—he paused to clear his throat and shake out the sleeves of his white robe—"let's get this game underway."

Ross glanced down at his watch. "I have exactly one hour and forty-five minutes before I'm due in at the station." He was dressed in most of his armor, save for the crested helmet he'd hung on one of the hooks near the bar.

"Bummer," Kevin said, fingering the rim of his Ambrosia Ale bottle. He hadn't taken a single sip since I arrived, but I had a feeling that had more to do with Ross's presence. He'd been the one to arrest Kevin when he'd been screwed up on hellfire, and even though Kevin was clean now, he'd retained a certain level of nervousness around Ross. He wore his work robe, and I suspected it was to hide a ragged band tee shirt beneath.

Abe grinned. "I'm prepared to see this game to its brutal end. It's my night off."

Gabriel smacked the deck down in front of Kevin for him to cut, and then he proceeded to deal. His eyes kept slipping toward me, and it took a minute before I realized he was fretting over my unusual silence.

I couldn't come right out and tell him what was on my mind, not in front of everyone else, so I decided to be extra interested in the pair of sixes I'd been dealt. I'd already tossed in a chip for the small blind, so I had to wait my turn to bid.

The new Texas hold 'em setup was thanks to Kevin. The Muses Union House had reopened over the summer, and to show our support we'd hired them to upgrade our card nights with a fancy set of custom poker chips. The tokens were stamped with the Death Deck's suit logos—lost souls for the white ten-dollar pieces, scythes for the gray twenty-five-dollar pieces, wilting daisies for the red fifty-dollar pieces, and coffins for the black one-hundred-dollar pieces.

When everyone had tossed in their two lost souls, and the betting circled back to me, I added a second lost soul piece to even the pot and then chucked in two black coffins. Either I'd bluff my way into some extra coin tonight, or I'd be out early and free to wander off with my troubled thoughts until I could get Gabriel alone.

The hull of the ship creaked softly as the sea rocked against it, and a salty breeze slipped through the open windows. It was a perfect night, only made better by the appearance of a young John Wayne, watching us from the muted television in his debut film, *The Big Trail*.

I waited as everyone silently debated what to do with their hands. Abe folded, staying true to his plan to stay in the game as long as possible. Ross went ahead and matched my bet. Kevin, too. Gabriel made a conflicted face before tossing his cards down. He grumbled and gave me the hairy eyeball before dealing out the first three community cards of the flop. I tried to keep a neutral expression as another six was placed face-up on the table, along with a four and an eight.

"All in," I said, nudging my stack of chips forward with the backs of both hands.

Abe's eyebrows shot up. "Jesus in a jumpsuit! Boy, am I glad to be out of this round."

Ross rubbed his chin a moment and stared down at the cards in his other hand. He squinted at me as if trying to determine whether or not I should be taken seriously. Then he sighed and folded. Kevin matched me without hesitation. Either he had a five and a seven in his hand, or he was as eager as I was to be pardoned from the game.

Gabriel's wings fluttered, and he scooted closer to the table as he picked up the deck. "All right, then. No more betting if you're both all in. Let's see those cards."

I laid down my sixes. The color drained from Kevin's face as he placed a four and an eight on the table. Two pairs—or a pile-up as we called it when playing with the Death Deck—was a decent enough hand. Maybe not a hand that most would go all-in with, but I'd seen it win a time or two. My own hand, a three of a kind *slash* drowning, wasn't much stronger. But that's why they called it a bluff.

Gabriel dealt out the fourth and fifth community cards, and I was done for when another eight appeared, promoting Kevin's two pairs to a better full house than my hand.

"Lost at sea!" he cheered.

I shrugged and gave him a small smile. "Good game."

I hung around for another few rounds, trying to be sociable, before excusing myself and heading up to the main deck for some fresh air. I sipped on an Ambrosia Ale as I absently checked over all the rigging and sails. Night had fallen fully by now, and the lanterns along the dock pier burned brightly, their white-hot light mingling with the golden glow from the lamps scattered around the ship's deck.

In the distance, I could see the yellow treetops over the city park, the spotlights surrounding the memorial garden reaching up through the leaves. A few more blocks to the west, Reapers Inc. marked the peak of the cityscape, with its seventy-five floors of glass windows. Random lights were on throughout the building, making it look like a monster-sized Jenga tower.

"Howdy, pilgrim," Gabriel said as he joined me, handing over a fresh Ambrosia Ale. He clinked the neck of his bottle against mine and took a long drink before folding his arms over the deck railing beside me. "What's on your mind?"

That was the million-dollar question. The answer could have taken all night, but I settled for the most condensed version I could manage. "Vince Hare is alive." I sighed and took a drink.

Gabriel's eyes widened as he blinked at me, the lanterns reflecting brightly in his pupils. He blew out a slow breath.

"You didn't know?" I squinted at him, trying to decide if he was genuinely shocked or faking it to cover for Saul. They'd been friends, centuries before I came along.

Gabriel shook his head. "I didn't." Then he frowned and finally looked at me. "How do you know for sure?"

"I ran into him on the mortal side yesterday."

That drew an even bigger reaction out of him. His wings fluttered as he stood up taller and turned in a tight circle, taking another drink from his ale.

"Grim sent Saul to take him out," I added, instantly picking up on his lack of surprise. A bug tickled my cheek as it flew by, and I shooed it away.

"I know," Gabriel admitted, pausing to give me a meaningful look. "I know, and I thought he had."

"Why didn't anyone tell me?" I asked, trying to keep the anger out of my voice.

Gabriel looked away and sighed again. "Vince was your classmate, and Saul didn't want you to hold it against him. It was a direct order, and not one he looked forward to carrying out. *Obviously*, since he didn't." He snorted and propped a hand on his robe-covered hip. The gesture reminded me of Peter, but I bit my tongue rather than say so. Gabriel would not find that amusing.

I turned and leaned my back and one elbow against the deck railing as I tilted my bottle up again. "Jenni doesn't believe me—or rather, she's worried about it getting back to the council."

"I bet." He ran a hand through his mess of blond curls and gave me a sympathetic smile. "Ridwan might have failed at having you terminated, but he's gaining ground with his campaign to have the Special Ops Unit dissolved."

"That figures." I rolled my eyes. "But it doesn't change the fact that I saw Vince yesterday, and he's snatching up souls for some reason or another."

Gabriel frowned and tapped his bottle of ale against his thigh. It was nearly empty. Mine, too. The conversation had driven us both to stress drinking, and we were no wiser for it.

"Do you think Saul might be alive, too?" I asked after a tense moment of silence.

"No." Gabriel shook his head. "I saw…what was left of him." He swallowed, and his eyes unfocused as his gaze dropped to the deck floor. "He was distant those last few years, and I wondered more than once if his death was as simple as the papers tried to make it sound."

"Simple?" I took a shaky breath, trying to decide what I wanted more. To know the truth or to hold fast to the righteous image I'd had of my mentor for all these decades.

Another stretch of silence followed before Gabriel found his bearings again. "Let this one go, Lana. You've been under enough fire for one century." His eyes drew up to meet mine, pleading. "You don't have to solve all of Eternity's problems."

A dry laugh slipped from me. "It would help if those problems didn't always land on my doorstep."

He gave me a lopsided grin. "Then don't answer the door."

CHAPTER TEN

"To witness two lovers is a spectacle for the gods."
—*Johann Wolfgang von Goethe*

Everyone had turned in for the night by the time I made it home. The hounds were curled up together on the new doggie bed I'd ordered from Hades' Hound House, and Bub was tucked in the enormous, king-sized bed in the center of our bedroom. Soft snores echoed off the vaulted ceiling as I slipped into a pair of pajama shorts and a tank top.

When I crawled under the sheets and pressed my cheek against Bub's back, curling my arms around his broad shoulders, he rotated in my embrace. His hands slipped around my hips and he pulled me in closer, crushing my chest to his. My heart thrummed happily, and I knew as long as every day ended like this, I could suffer through just about anything.

Bub's breath grazed my cheek, and then one of his hands cradled my head, and our lips met.

"Did you rob them all blind, my sweet?" he whispered as he pulled away.

I trembled with a silent laugh, not wanting to wake the hounds. "I went down in a blaze of glory with my first hand."

"That's unfortunate. I should have one of my winged minions help you cheat next time." My breath hitched, and I noticed the corners of his mouth tighten in the faint light provided by the stars sparkling through the skylight overhead. The glimpse of the mortal world was an enchantment on the estate that had survived through the riots and destruction of the original manor, and it made me feel like we were trapped between the two worlds in a pocket of space made just for us.

"Your minions were less subtle today," I whispered, skipping right over the polite question I usually asked. I was too tired to play stupid.

"I was trying to keep you out of trouble, love," Bub said, rubbing a hand down my back. "Not that their gentle warnings did any good."

"I do what I want," I replied. It was almost playful, but I'd meant it.

Bub grinned. "This I know." Then his eyes leveled with mine and grew serious. "But I do hope you're being careful with whom you trust your secrets to. The council's attention grows more dangerous all the time. We've both had close calls with their wrath, and I fear our luck will run out if we continue to test it."

I frowned and avoided his stare by tucking my chin over his shoulder, snuggling in closer. I didn't want to argue. I just wanted the comfort of his warm skin against mine.

Our hips knocked together, sending a fluttering sensation through my middle. Bub drew in a deep breath as if he felt it, too. He flexed his torso, angling his hips and then thrusting them against mine again, drawing an agreeable sound from me.

I gasped as he gripped my arms and rolled onto his back, hoisting me into the air above him. His fingers slipped under the hem of my shirt, sliding up until the material was bunched over my breasts, and I shuddered blissfully. He laughed as I yanked the tank top off and threw it across the room. Then he pulled me down for another kiss before knotting his hands in the thin material of my shorts. I moved to take them off, but he held me in place, his lips trailing the side of my throat as I writhed against him.

"Let me enjoy you, love," he whispered. "We have all the time in the world."

I groaned in protest but let him take the lead anyway. I knew how this would end, if the anticipation didn't kill me first. Bub was a master tease, and he loved to hear me beg.

Making love to my skilled demon was always a good distraction from my worries. But a few hours later, after being thoroughly ravished, I found myself lying awake in bed. Yet again.

Bub's arm stretched across my stomach. His head rested on my shoulder, and his cool breath rushed over my naked chest, curling up the side of my neck. I combed my fingers through the shorter hairs at the base of his skull, stiff with dried sweat, and worried over the things I hadn't shared with him yet.

Some part of Naledi's procedure had failed. She had to know this, and it angered me that she'd intentionally left my fate in such a volatile condition. Hadn't I been through enough due to the details of my creation that I'd had no control over? She was the only one I could talk openly to about the unresolved matter, and I intended to visit her after work on Wednesday. There was just the trouble of getting Bub's buggish detail to buzz off.

The other person I wanted to pay a visit to would be a bit harder to track down. I cringed as I thought about the extra coin it was going to cost me, especially after I'd wracked my brain to figure out how to budget in the coin it would require to travel to the throne realm. It still didn't add up to the amount it would cost to drag the hounds along for my harvests all day. Of course, I only needed Saul. Maybe Coreen could spend the day on the ship with the helljacks.

My mind continued racing, waking me up off and on all night. So many faces haunted my dreams—Saul, Vince, Grim, Seth, Ridwan, Josie, Adrianna—the list went on and on. I felt entirely defeated when orange morning light washed the stars from the sky.

I slipped out of bed without waking Bub and found my shorts and tank top before making my way downstairs to the kitchen. I needed coffee. Lots of it.

The manor's kitchen was decked out with all the newest gadgets and gizmos. It was a gourmet chef's wet dream, but all I cared about was the coffeemaker. I was sure Bub had it all set up and programmed to kick on soon, so I went ahead and pressed the brew button and waited patiently for the machine to do its magic. I was rewarded a few minutes later with a steaming cup of dark roast. I added a generous amount of peppermint creamer and took the cup out onto the patio.

Now that the daylight was returning, I could see the new developments in the garden. The landscapers had come as promised, and a stone wall outlined the perimeter. A walking path in matching stonework dissected the upturned earth, coiling and twisting in a labyrinthine pattern that Bub had designed himself. Now that the framework had been laid, he'd finally be able to start planting all the nightmarish seedlings he'd been harboring in our garage next to my motorcycle.

The French doors off the patio opened, and Bub stepped out to join me with his own cup of coffee. He'd pulled on a pair of shorts, but his chest was bare, displaying a small, circular bite mark I'd left over the swell of his right shoulder. My own shoulders shivered at the memory.

The hounds trailed after Bub. Saul pranced over to greet me, and Coreen yawned as she dipped her back into a deep stretch, pushing her paws out in front of her. When Saul finished having his ears scratched, he went to lie beside her—or rather, on top of her. He nipped playfully at her tail and pawed her muzzle when she tried to return the favor.

Bub cradled his mug of coffee in one hand and wrapped his other around my waist as he gazed out over the garden. "And now the fun begins," he said, a twinkle taking hold of his eyes.

"Oh, joy." I sipped my coffee, hoping the caffeine would translate into enough stamina to get me through the questionable day I'd laid out for myself. Bub's day would definitely be weirder than mine, planting bleeding fungus and voodoo lilies, but I envied him already.

If Jenni figured out what I was up to, she'd probably want to plant *me*. Right in the memorial garden alongside our fallen colleagues.

CHAPTER ELEVEN

*"It is better to conquer yourself than to win a thousand battles.
Then the victory is yours. It cannot be taken from you,
not by angels or by demons, heaven or hell."*
—*Buddha*

My second meeting with Regina did not yield a more favorable opinion, of her or me. I could tell she wasn't thrilled to see me again from the square of her shoulders and the slight twitch in her wings as I stepped off the elevator and into the lobby of Reapers Inc.

"Botch any dockets lately?" I asked, trying to see how long she could maintain the fake smile plastered across her face. When her jaw trembled, and her eyes began to well up, a stab of remorse took me by surprise. Schoolyard bully never looked good on anyone.

Regina pushed my harvest list, along with Ellen's and Kevin's, across the desk. "I double-checked everything twice," she said, quickly pulling her hand back as I reached for the documents.

"Thanks," I grumbled under my breath, feeling like a jackass for having no better reason to hate the girl than the fact that she hadn't mastered Ellen's job on her first day. As I turned away, she let out a small gasp.

"President Fang would like to see you this morning. I'll let her know you're here." She picked up her desk phone and pressed a button. I could hear the faint buzz of the intercom through Jenni's door. "Ms. Harvey has arrived. Yes, ma'am," Regina said into the phone. Then she hung up and gave me another forced smile. "She'll see you now."

I pressed my lips together and swallowed. My pulse beat more urgently against my temples as I entered Jenni's office. There was no reason to think she suspected me of anything, but I didn't exactly subdue guilt with much grace.

"Lana," Jenni greeted me without looking up from her desk. "Come on in and have a seat."

I closed the door behind me and stuffed the soul dockets clutched in my sweaty hand down inside my messenger bag as I crossed the room. The wall of glass behind Jenni's desk was filled with golden, morning light. It reflected off the Sea of Eternity in the distance and slowly crawled over the treetops as it moved inland, like a glass of orange juice spilling over the edge of a table. The sight of it calmed my nerves as I dropped down onto one of the leather benches and folded my hands in my lap.

Jenni flipped through a stack of stationery, occasionally pausing to scrawl her signature or initials on a blank line. Her wave of dark hair was pulled back tight into a French twist, and a pair of reading glasses perched on the end of her nose. She made me wait a few minutes longer before giving me her full attention. I wasn't sure if she was really *that* engrossed with her work, or if maybe she was getting used to throwing around her fancy new authority. She'd been taking more opportunities to flex her boss muscles around me lately, as if she were afraid I was plotting to take over.

I had thought Naledi's procedure would have done away with that sort of insecurity, but it only seemed to make it worse for Jenni. Like it was somehow proof that I was more. Sure, I was cut from a different cloth. It wasn't a secret any longer. But it shouldn't have been a problem either, now that I'd been *fixed*. What made me unique had been zapped by Naledi, the soul on the Throne of Eternity, and the only one with the ability to pull off such an inconceivable feat.

Maybe I was reading too much into Jenni's actions. It was also possible that our friendship was going through an odd transition since our joint living arrangement had ended.

"How's Ellen handling herself?" Jenni asked, fingering a Chinese knot button along her collarbone. Half a dozen more ran in a diagonal line across the corner of her white blouse.

"Okay, I guess," I answered with a short nod. "Though I think you should have her retake her L&L before setting her loose to harvest on her own."

Jenni's chin dimpled with a thoughtful frown. "Very good." She tapped the end of her ink pen on her desk and then pulled her hand up to rest her chin in her palm. "The council approved a new generation of reapers yesterday. Naledi is working on them now, before Ridwan manages to change everyone's minds."

I resisted rolling my eyes and tried to smile. "Two years since the Ks came aboard. Wow."

The first eleven generations were all equally spaced a century apart, but casualties of war had taken a bite out of our numbers. Reaping had become more burdensome for everyone, and while I was sure that Jenni's retirement plans had smoothed many a frazzled nerve over the mess, I didn't see how it would end well if things didn't improve soon. The council would never allow a reaper to retire if it put the soul harvesting industry in a bind.

Jenni watched me carefully as she shared her next bit of news. "The Special Ops Unit is officially dissolved."

I bit my bottom lip and then scoffed. "Ridwan?"

She nodded grimly. "It's a balancing act, working with the council. Give and take."

"Right." The word sounded more resigned than the loathing sarcasm I was going for.

Jenni cleared her throat and began tidying her paperwork. "I haven't seen your application for the Posy Unit cross my desk."

"I haven't decided if that's what I want to do." I tangled my fingers in the strap of my messenger bag. "Kevin's benefiting from the random freelance work. The pay is shit," I said, casting her a scornful look before I went on. "But the diversity of harvests is expanding his experience rather quickly."

Jenni cocked her head to one side. "You're actually very good as a mentor, you know?" Her pen tapped out another staccato tune. "You should consider teaching at the academy again. They're going to need the help, now that we have *two* young generations to mold into respectable reapers."

"Yeah, maybe." I sighed and glanced out the window again, noticing the movement of the sea as the morning tide churned and sprayed up over the lip of the harbor sea wall.

The Three Fates Factory workday would begin soon. My workday needed to kick off too, especially if I wanted to manage all the illegal activity I had planned.

"Good catching up," Jenni said with a polite yet dismissive nod, as if she'd forgotten our previous, less friendly conversation that had taken place two days before. She hadn't mentioned my sighting of Vince, and she seemed relieved that I hadn't either. I'd let her keep the pet elephant in the room. For now.

I left Reapers Inc. in a hurry and took the travel booths to the harbor. The morning was lovely, and I would have liked to enjoy it with a stroll through the city, but there was no time. I pulled the soul dockets out of my messenger bag and then dug deeper until I felt the brimstone gun. Bub had taken it off Tasha Henry last spring when we'd tracked her down. And now I was going to use it to track her down again.

Saul reared back on his hind legs and flopped his front paws over the deck railing as I climbed the ramp to my ship. The two helljacks tried to mimic him, though they were a bit smaller than their uncle. Their narrower muzzles rested between their paws, and one chomped down on the railing as I came aboard.

"Hey!" I shouted, sending them all off in a lap around the forecastle.

Coreen watched from the upper deck with a bored expression. She'd gotten lazy since weaning the helljacks, but I could hardly blame her. She deserved the break after rearing her rambunctious lot. Her third pup had been adopted by Apollo and the Pythia, and thank goodness. I couldn't imagine

Coreen fending off all three of them once they'd reached their current size.

Kevin stepped out of his cabin, rubbing a towel over his freshly shaved face. "You're early," he said, then jumped back as the trio of demonic pooches ran past.

I glared after them. "You need better dog toys. I caught one of your heathens chewing on the ship."

Kevin made an uncomfortable face. "Yeah, I know. I had to replace one of the rigging ropes, too. I'm hoping this phase passes soon."

I resisted chewing him a new asshole and thrust his docket out instead. "Here. You're taking Ellen on your first run."

"What?" he balked. "Why?"

"Because I'm the mentor, and I say so," I snapped, then added more gently, "I have a solo job to take care of, but I'll be back soon. It's one run, Kevin. You can handle it."

"Fine." He huffed and took the list from me.

I patted my leg and whistled for Saul to come, drawing a confused look from Kevin.

"You're taking Saul? What about Coreen?"

I shook my head. "She can stay here with the pups, maybe keep them from destroying everything while I'm gone." I raised an eyebrow at him and then headed for the ramp to the dock pier. I wanted to be gone before Ellen showed up and I was forced to repeat my weak ruse. She'd be harder to appease with the mentor card, seeing as how she was seven hundred years older than I was.

A handful of reapers were scattered down the dock pier, some getting an early start on the day's harvests, and others sharing coffee or doing maintenance on their boats. I spotted Arden Faraji's shiny, bald head as he climbed the ratlines of his own ship, anchored across the way. He straddled a yard and made an adjustment to some rigging along the center mast.

Arden was doing a bang-up job with the Posy Unit. Definitely a better job than I'd done. I didn't have any doubt that he'd be a decent boss if I decided to apply to rejoin the unit like Jenni had suggested. But the idea of having a supervisor, no matter how fair or friendly they were, just seemed like another rung down on the ladder I'd spent the past two years climbing. I intended to hold off for as long as possible, or at least until the shitty paychecks finally succeeded in destroying what was left of my ego.

The carousel centered on the main deck of Arden's ship moved suddenly, carnival music and bright lights encouraging the painted horses to begin their slow march. The machine's function served to not only entertain the child souls Arden and his partner were so fond of, but it was also hooked into the rigging and made for smoother sailing. It was smart, even if a bit strange.

Arden's eyes fell on me as he turned to descend, and he waved. I returned the gesture and nudged my leg against Saul's side as I rolled my coin, trading my occupational concerns for more dire ones as I disappeared to the mortal realm.

CHAPTER TWELVE

*"When one jumps over the edge, one is bound to land some-
where."*
—*D.H. Lawrence*

I didn't notice the fly clinging to the sleeve of my robe until
the sun blinded me as I appeared on the rocky beach of Fort
Zachary Taylor in Key West. I lifted my arm up to shield my
eyes, and an unmistakable buzz filled my ears.

Instinctively, I smacked my hands together, squashing the
bug between my palms. Bub was not going to be happy.

I groaned as I wiped the bug guts off on my robe and
then quickly dug the brimstone pistol out of my bag. I needed
to get out of here before Bub sent another of his spies. Saul
tilted his muzzle up and crinkled his nose at the rotten egg
smell coming from the powder around the lip of the gun's
barrel. I held it closer.

"You got it?" I asked, letting him get a good sniff. When
he pressed his nose to the ground and took off, I chased after
him, excitement bubbling in my chest. "Good boy!"

We cut inland, heading away from the shore and toward
a small patch of trees. The tip of the island was narrow, and I
could hear the ocean on the opposite side as we approached.
This was the last place Tasha had been spotted. I'd heard Clair

Kramer, Grace Adaline's apprentice, reported the sighting after harvesting a soul off the coast. He hadn't actually seen Tasha, but rather her yacht anchored to one of the human piers. A few nephilim guards had been sent to investigate, but they came back empty-handed.

I didn't expect to find Tasha on the island. If Saul could suss out where she'd been staying, I was hoping we'd find some clue as to where she might have headed. When I spied her yacht anchored out near the shore, I almost did a cartwheel. I never got this lucky.

My and Saul's thrashing around through the trees was none too quiet, and as we stepped out onto the sandy beach, movement caught my eye. Right before a fist did.

"Gah!" I shrieked, stumbling backward and tripping over my robe. My ass hit the sand. Saul didn't even give a warning growl before leaping over me and taking my attacker down.

"Truce! Truce!" Tasha cried.

"Sure. *Now,* you want a truce." I sat up straighter and touched my tender eye socket. "Jerk," I added as an afterthought. "I came here bearing gifts, too."

Tasha laughed, but it sounded strange since Saul was standing on her chest. "I'd settle for not having my throat ripped out."

I made a face at her but then nodded at Saul, giving him the cue to let her go.

"Thanks." Tasha sat up slowly and coughed into the bend of her elbow as she regained her breath. She didn't look too bad for being a wanted fugitive living in exile on the mortal side. Her hair was longer than when I'd last seen her, almost reaching her jawline, and paired with her cut-off shorts and lime green bikini top, she looked like she was on vacation.

"I like this look much better than the demon rocker guise you were sporting," I said, waving my hand at her. "Speaking of demons, where's Tack?" I glanced through the trees behind her and then across the open beach.

Tasha's lips pursed, and I noticed the scars nested in her dimples from where she'd taken out her piercings. "Who knows where that loser ran off to? We parted ways several months ago, in Nebraska, after he blamed me for everything rotten that's ever happened to him. Is that my gun?" Her eyes blinked wildly as I lifted the pistol, as if she hadn't expected to ever see it again.

"Yup. I thought you might like it back—though I really hope you don't have to use it."

Her brow scrunched. "Why would I?"

"You were spotted," I said, drawing a small gasp from her. "On the other side of this beach."

"But I haven't been here in over a week. I just got back," she insisted.

"Guess that's why the Nephilim Guard didn't find you when they were sent to investigate." I shrugged and dropped the gun in the sand between us. "I'd find a new beach if I were you. In case they've been ordered to keep an eye on this spot."

"Great." She pulled her legs up and rested her elbows on her knees with a sigh. "And I really liked this particular corner of the world. I knew I should have waited for the off season."

"There's always the Red Sand Beach in Maui," I suggested.

Tasha gave me a sly grin. "Something tells me you didn't come all the way out here to return my gun and talk hideout options."

"Who needs small talk anyway, right?" I returned her grin, thankful for the directness and lack of sass she was so well known for. "You're not the only reaper living on the mortal fringe," I said, trying to gauge her reaction. Her surprise seemed genuine enough, so I went on. "Vince Hare is alive, and he's been hiding among the mortals for the last century."

Tasha's eyes bulged, and she leaned back as if I'd struck her. "What?"

"It gets better. One of the missing factory workers that wasn't recovered last spring is helping him poach souls—and not just any souls, original believers like Naledi, the one on the throne."

"That doesn't make any sense." She shook her head. "I've bumped into a few demons on this side, and all of them say the ghost market is dead."

I held my breath a moment and chewed my bottom lip. "Then he's keeping them somewhere on this side. Though, for what purpose, I don't know."

Tasha fingered her bangs out of her face and turned her worried eyes to the ocean. "Why tell me all this?"

And here came the tricky part I'd been dreading. "I need your help finding them."

She'd been expecting my answer, and her poker face was top-notch. "What's in it for me?"

I took a deep breath through my nose and then pushed it past my lips. "Name your price." If any cause was worthy of cracking open my nest egg, it was this.

Tasha's stony expression went slack, and she gave me a sad smile. "You helped me escape the council's noose, and now you've given me a heads-up about the guard. I really am an ungrateful lout, aren't I?"

I shrugged, not wanting to outright agree with her, but also not prepared to deny it. That earned me a laugh.

"Fine," Tasha said. "I'll ask around, but I only have a few contacts on this side. Don't be surprised if no leads turn up."

"Your nothing can't be any worse than the nothing I'm currently working with." I stood and dusted the sand from my robe.

Tasha stood too, but she ignored the grains clinging to her. She was probably used to it by now. She picked up the brimstone gun and looked it over with a small grin before tucking it in the waistband of her jean shorts.

"There's a bar in Jamaica where the locals like to go cliff diving," she said. "They close up shop around ten, so no accidental deaths or reapers should show after that. Want to meet me there around eleven tonight?"

"Sure." I nodded, mentally working out a plan to show up an hour early and case the spot. I didn't want any surprise deaths mucking up our rendezvous.

"Also…" Tasha dug her hand down in one of her front pockets. "Since you were nice enough to return my gun, I guess I should give this back."

She pulled out the skeleton coin that Naledi had slipped me before my hearing with the council last spring. I'd thought Naledi intended for me to use it to escape, in the event that the council ordered my termination. But when they decided to let me live, I'd used it to help Tasha escape her cell at the Nephilim Guard Station. Her verdict hadn't been so nice, and while we were far from besties, I didn't think she deserved to die for her crimes.

I took the coin and held it up in the sun to get a better look. "Thanks."

"Even?" Tasha asked. She was grinning, but I could tell she wanted us to be square, that it was important to her.

"Even Steven."

I took down the Jamaican bar information, and then Saul and I didn't waste any more time heading to the harbor in Limbo City. I imagined that both Kevin and Ellen were cursing my name. Not to mention the Lord of the Flies.

I grimaced as I thought about the earful I'd likely get later for smashing Bub's minion. But to be fair, no one had ever accused me of being the kind of person who wouldn't harm a fly.

CHAPTER THIRTEEN

"Jupiter from on high smiles at the perjuries of lovers."
—*Ovid*

As soon as I made it back to Limbo, my phone began to ring. Bub left two very heated messages, and then Ellen called from home, explaining that she needed a fresh change of clothes due to a lagoon incident on the mortal side. She also tearfully reiterated how much she missed her desk. When I finally let her go, Kevin was waiting to tell me off, threatening to burn the ship down before taking Ellen with him on another harvest.

I promised never again, and then tried to put Tasha and our Jamaica date out of my mind so I could focus on the day's harvests. I let Bub wait until my lunch break, when I managed to steal five minutes of privacy in the bowels of the ship, before calling him back. Groveling was bad enough without an audience.

"Don't you understand?" he fumed in my ear. "They're not just my underlings. They're a part of *me*. You smashed *me*."

I rolled my eyes. He made it sound like I was murdering babies or something. "You don't sound smashed," I muttered under my breath.

"What was that?"

"You're absolutely right." I recovered quickly. "I'm so sorry. It was a reflex. I don't know what I was thinking—maybe I wasn't thinking at all."

"You're humoring me now," Bub grumbled on the other end of the line. "And you're not doing a very convincing job of hiding it."

"What can I do to make it up to you?" I asked in a more heartfelt tone.

"I could use a hand with the bleeding fungus." The mischievous note in his reply told me I was already forgiven, though I was glad he couldn't see the face I made.

"Can it wait until tomorrow? I've made plans with Ellen tonight, and they might run a bit late," I added, remembering my eleven o'clock with Tasha.

Bub huffed. "Fine, but I expect to have you all to myself tomorrow evening."

"Deal."

I wasn't looking forward to playing in the mud with all the creepy crawlies, but the promise of another bubble bath would get me through it. Bub and I said our goodbyes, and I made my way upstairs to the main deck.

Ellen and Kevin were eating street tacos on opposite ends of the ship. They weren't talking to one another. The details of the morning harvest I had missed were a little fuzzy, though it should have been an easy enough job. The two souls they'd collected were in crappy moods, too. I'd peeked in on them earlier, before sneaking off to call Bub, and caught them glaring at each other as they paced amongst the rest of the souls in the cargo hold.

I grabbed the taco Kevin brought back for me and found a neutral spot in the center of the deck, atop the closed hatch platform, where I could eat without having my loyalties questioned. A horn echoed across the sea from the Three Fates Factory, signaling the end of their lunch hour. It made me eat faster, even though I didn't have to punch a timecard. These souls weren't going to reap themselves.

Kevin finished his lunch first and made the mistake of dropping his last taco wrapper to the deck floor. The helljacks appeared out of nowhere, snatching it up and tearing it to shreds in a matter of seconds. I would have complained about the mess, but there wasn't one. They didn't just lap up the cheese and sour cream residue. They *ate* the wrapper.

"I'm outta here," Kevin said, pulling on his work robe again. Tacos were messy, and the laundromat was not his most favorite place to hang out after work.

I held my half-eaten taco up. "Thanks for lunch."

"Your turn tomorrow," he reminded me. Then he pointed his hounds over to where Coreen was chewing on a charred hellcat bone. It was one of the few treats she could enjoy without having to share with her brood. The helljacks' diets were atrocious, and they'd devour almost anything. *Anything*. But for some reason, they couldn't stand the taste of hellcat. They plopped down on the deck a safe distance from the offending treat and watched as Kevin disappeared down the ramp. The smaller of the two dogs let out a soft, mournful howl.

Ellen waited until Kevin had blipped out of sight before joining me on the hatch platform. The glamorous, retro curls she usually sported were missing. Instead, her hair was pulled back in a messy ponytail with bits of frizz poking out here and there. I had a feeling the new look had something to do with the botched morning harvest, so I refrained from asking about it.

"That apprentice of yours has quite the mouth on him," she said, wadding up her taco wrapper and stuffing it down inside the empty box on the platform behind us.

"You have no idea." I wiped my hands off on my jeans, having shed my robe like Kevin, and then closed up the box of taco trash. The helljacks watched me eagerly.

"Are you still up for Athena's after work?" Ellen asked as we gathered up our things and headed for the dock pier. Saul napped near the ramp, but he looked up when he heard us approaching.

"*Manto*," I said to him and bent to scratch his ears before replying to Ellen. "Yeah, definitely."

My bank account would have disagreed, but I could tell Ellen and I both needed this. The sausage fest poker party had made me painfully aware of my lack of girlfriends, and as sorry as I felt for myself over my work situation, Ellen's was much worse.

"So, who else are we shuffling off the mortal coil today?" she asked, tossing our trash into a bin as we reached the dock.

I dug our dockets out of my bag and glanced over them, scratching my head. "Lots of shitty drivers and a handful of earthquake leftovers."

Ellen's nose crinkled. "I thought the Recovery Unit was supposed to take care of all of those."

"Yeah, well, sometimes a few slip by. They're easier to collect after the humans send in their emergency responders." I liked it when the mortals made my job easier.

A few storks from the factory hopped along the pier, throwing their heads back and clattering their bills as they enjoyed the cool breeze coming in off the sea. Ellen gave them a longing look as she pulled her coin from her pocket.

"I should check on Duster again before we head to Athena's later," she said.

I gave her a strained smile, hoping she wouldn't invite me along for that particular errand, and fetched my own coin. Birds weren't my favorite, and Duster was the worst.

The rest of the workday was boring. Too boring. My mind skipped back and forth between Saul's death and Vince's current motives. I had to know if they were related, even if no one else seemed to think it mattered. Also, I wanted to find the rest of the missing souls, and then I wanted to rub them in Ridwan's face for shutting down my fledgling unit prematurely.

The self-gratifying fantasy was playing on a loop in my mind when Ellen and I made our pit stop at her apartment. Ellen pushed her front door open wide and waved her arm at me as she stepped inside.

"Make yourself at home," she said, ignoring Duster's squawking protests from his cage in the corner of her living room. His colorful wings fanned out behind him as his chest bumped against the bars in a threatening show of dominance.

"Yeesh. Chillax, Tweety," I said, venturing a few feet inside the room.

The apartments at Reapers Tower were nice. Not Holly House nice, but definitely the next best thing when it came to living in Limbo. A faux stone fireplace with a glossy walnut mantel stretched across one wall, and matching woodwork lined the bay window in the dining room. The theme continued in the kitchen with stone-patterned linoleum and walnut cabinets.

Ellen cooed at Duster as she filled a small dish with seeds and berries. I cringed when she cracked open the cage door to slip the dish inside. If that thing got loose, I was making a run for it. Duster made one last squawk before turning his attention away from me and attacking a blueberry. A red feather drifted between the bars of the cage and landed atop a pile of newspapers spread out on the carpet below.

Ellen picked it up and added it to a collection of filled vases next to a stack of library books about coin travel on her dining room table. When she caught my quizzical expression, she laughed. "The crones at the market buy the feathers from me—but only after Duster reaches adulthood," she said as she stripped out of her work robe. "They can't pass them off as authentic phoenix feathers since he's a toy breed hybrid, but they can use them in some of their crafts."

"Making him earn his keep, eh?" I set my messenger bag down on a small table near the front door so I could peel off my robe. I wadded it up and tucked it down inside my bag, which was lighter now without the weight of Tasha's brimstone pistol.

I stole a quick glance at the grandfather clock in the corner opposite Duster's cage before we left the apartment. I was supposed to be in Jamaica in five hours, where I'd hopefully learn something useful.

"I'm thinking leggings," Ellen said as we headed for the elevator at the end of the hall.

"Hmm?" I said, my mind elsewhere.

"Leggings," Ellen repeated. "You know, stretchy pants?"

"Right! Right." I forced a smile. "Perfect for fall weather. Comfy, too."

She pursed her lips and frowned as we stepped into an empty elevator. "Is everything all right, sweetie? You've been awfully distracted today."

I sighed and wrapped my hands around the strap of my messenger bag where it lay at an angle over my chest. "Bub and I are fighting," I said dejectedly.

It wasn't an outright lie, but I knew it would be enough to evoke some sympathy from Ellen. Her sudden gasp was right on cue.

"What happened?"

"I smashed one of his flies—totally on accident." Okay. That was stretching the truth a bit.

Ellen made a gagging face and shuddered as the elevator doors slid open in the lobby. She was still doing her heebie-jeebies dance after we'd left the building and walked around the block to the travel booth on the corner of Council Street and Tombstone Drive.

I had almost suggested we walk, but reaping required a lot more physical activity than Ellen's former desk job, and she was still getting used to it. Also, Athena's was located in the heart of the historic district, so no matter where the booths spit us out, we had another two blocks ahead of us.

Athena didn't spend much time at her boutique these days, not since taking Horus's spot on the Afterlife Council. Instead of being waist-deep in fashion, she was now neck-deep in politics. What a trade-off. Her enchanted wooden dummies were on duty though, along with Arachne, who somehow had even *less* personality than a dummy. The girl didn't even look up from her magazine as Ellen and I entered the dress shop.

"Welcome to Athena's," she said dryly, not even bothering to recite the seasonal greeting I was sure Athena had made her memorize.

A pair of dummies in posh business suits stood on one of the circular display platforms. They each held a clipboard, and as Ellen and I approached them, they handed us a sheet of coupons for the fall sale.

"Ha!" Ellen slapped the back of her hand against the page and turned it to me. "See? Leggings." Her eyes lit up as she wandered over to a rack of colorful tights. I reluctantly followed.

My wardrobe had been rather mute lately. Blood and guts were easier to wash out of black. But I hadn't seen much bloodshed since the ghost market shut down and the rest of the demon rebels finally slunk off to the shadows. Maybe I could benefit from a little bedazzling.

I fingered through a row of silk blouses while Ellen went to try on a pair of cheetah print tights. An emerald green number with a plunging neckline caught my attention, but after checking the price tag, I changed my mind.

I huffed out a gloomy sigh and made my way over to a rack of clearance scarves. A dummy with a dozen draped over each of her wooden arms danced excitedly as I neared, and I humored her by selecting a blue scarf dotted with dragonflies from her collection.

"These are amazing," Ellen said, holding up a second and third pair of tights when she caught up with me. "I need a pair in every color. Ooh, heels!" She gasped and snatched up a pair of glittery red stilettos. "Do you think these go with the cheetah?" she asked, holding the two items against each other.

"Under a black robe, everything matches." My laughter cut off when Ellen's smile wavered. "But for a night out, sure. It looks great," I said, giving her a pained smile.

"Who am I kidding," Ellen moaned. "I'll never be seen in anything cute again." She dropped the heels on the rack she'd found them on, discarding the tights along with them. A dummy appeared to put everything back in its rightful place.

"Come on now," I said, summoning a cheerful voice. I grabbed the tights and fought off the mannequin as it tried to take them from me. "I bet you'll have lots of opportunities to wear these. Coffee dates and poker games. Hey, you could be wearing them right now even."

"Yeah?" Ellen said, raising an eyebrow hopefully.

"Definitely." I draped the tights over her arm. "Come check out the scarves. They're on sale."

Ellen's mood perked again as we continued our shopping, and I did a better job of keeping my foot out of my mouth. Just because I was broke and depressed about my job dilemma didn't mean I needed to bring her down in the dumps with me.

When we paid for our items and headed outside, I spotted a tiny fly buzzing around the ivy that climbed up the face of the building. Bub was at it again, but at least he was being more subtle this time and not having his minion buzz around in my face. I suspected that would start back up once he realized I intended to visit Naledi.

I'd just have to lose him before then.

CHAPTER FOURTEEN

"Only the dead have seen the end of war."
—*George Santayana*

Ellen and I took our time heading back to her apartment, ducking inside several more stores in the historic district as daylight faded, and the city lights slowly flickered to life. We also paused at the Phantom Café and grabbed some hot chocolate, but we stepped out onto the sidewalk to enjoy it, where a factory soul with a battered violin busked near a travel booth.

The girl looked familiar, and I wondered if I had harvested her at some point. Her shapeless, green dress and white go-go boots looked like they'd come straight from the sixties. Watching her made me think of Ruth, and I wondered if they'd known each other. Was the sad melody she played in memory of a lost friend? I tossed a coin into her case before Ellen and I rode the booths across town.

The Lord of the Flies' minion managed to slip in with us, though it lingered outside Reapers Tower, buzzing around a pot of mums, while I entered the building with Ellen. Bub must have figured that I was at least entitled to some private girl talk.

I went upstairs with Ellen and said goodbye at her front door, turning down her offer to stay for dinner. Duster was in the throes of a second tantrum, and I had somewhere to be. The skeleton coin Tasha had returned that morning was burning a hole in my pocket.

I waited until I was inside the elevator again, and then as the car descended toward the lobby, I dug the coin out and flipped it in the air, heading straight for the throne realm.

I wondered how long it would take for Bub to call and check up on me, but the thought quickly died as I took in Naledi's slice of Eternity. It felt strangely foreign under the pale light of dusk, though the sky was still brighter than Limbo City's.

The earth-contact homes built into the knolls surrounding Naledi's cottage were quaint. They looked like something straight out of a fairytale book, with thatched roofs and heavy wooden doors. Gardens, which dotted the landscape, stretched out before me, overflowing with flowers and produce. Now that the original believers and the throne realm were no longer a secret, a more natural light schedule had been implemented, opening up all kinds of possibilities. There was even a small orchard in a clearing between two of the houses.

I didn't have a formal invitation, and since I hadn't used the travel booths, I instead appeared in the open meadow that expanded to the outer edges of the small realm. A few startled faces gawked at me from oval windows in the hobbit-ish homes, and I began to question if I'd made a mistake showing up this way. The skeleton coin had helped me dodge Bub's detail, and I was also more than happy to save the extra coin the standard route would have cost, but none of that mattered if I couldn't secure a private audience with Naledi.

"You're late," Morgan, a young soul who had come over from Faerie to join Naledi's Apparition Agency, called out to me. She sat on a bench swing hanging off the cottage's front porch, her ankles crossed, and her feet tucked into Mary Janes. Red tights covered her legs under her black dress, and a matching red headband held back her short hair.

"When were you expecting me?" I asked, tightening my grip on the strap of my messenger bag as I climbed the stairs to escape all the prying eyes.

Morgan blinked a few times, making her look like a strange doll someone had forgotten on the porch after play-time. "Naledi thought you'd come yesterday," she said matter-of-factly.

"Is that so?" I rubbed my hands over the goosebumps spreading down my arms. Psychic predictions made my skin crawl.

Morgan hopped off the swing and opened the front door to the cottage. She tilted her head forward, encouraging me to enter when I didn't move right away. I pressed my lips together and tried to smile my thanks as I stepped into the foyer. The door slammed behind me, and I jumped, alarmed that she hadn't followed me inside.

For all the changes in the throne realm, the cottage was quite familiar, even in the broodier evening light that filtered down from the domed glass ceiling. The stone walls were bare, and the same burner that Winston had filled with exotic herbs and incense in his attempt to woo Naledi hung in one corner. It looked dusty and unused, causing my heart to tighten with a million turbulent emotions.

"Lana," Naledi greeted me from the arched entrance to the living room. A beige dress draped over one of her shoulders and wrapped around her middle before dropping in a smooth line all the way to the floor. The material was rugged, like burlap potato sacks, but the way she wore it suggested royalty. It was nicer than the rags she'd been wearing when I'd harvested her, and she seemed way more comfortable than she'd been in the fancy dress suits Jenni had tried to convince her to wear to win the council's approval.

"You look well," I said, taking in her bright eyes and the coil of smooth braids tied in a low knot at the base of her neck.

She spared me a polite nod of thanks. "I've been expecting you."

"So I heard." I gave her a nervous smile and let her lead me around the corner to one of the sofas in the living room. When I sat down, I pulled my bag onto my lap and fiddled nervously with the buckles along the front pocket. The television Winston had so loved was draped with a sheet of white silk, and it startled me even more so than the incense burner had.

"Would you like something to drink?" Naledi asked, folding her hands over her knees.

"No thanks. I really can't stay long."

She gasped softly. "That's right. You have an appointment to keep."

I felt my face warm, and my skin began to crawl again. "So, do you know why I'm here? God, I don't even know where to begin right now." It was hard telling how awkward this conversation was going to get. I hated not knowing what she knew via her special throne powers.

Naledi gave me an apologetic smile and patted my leg. "Sorry. I'm working on my bedside manner. It's harder than you'd think, given my condition. Please, start wherever you'd like to."

My brow pinched, and I wet my lips, trying to gather my thoughts now that her weird all-knowing mojo had thrown me off. "Vince Hare, a reaper who was supposedly terminated some time ago, is alive, and he's snatching up souls on the mortal side."

Naledi nodded as I spoke, and I wasn't sure if it was to show that she was listening or to convey that she already knew all of this. When she didn't say anything, I went on.

"Saul Avelo, my late mentor, was ordered to terminate Vince. But he didn't."

"And now you want to know why," Naledi said. She'd stated it like a fact rather than a question, but I felt compelled to answer anyway.

"Yes." I waited, thinking she was about to tell me, but her gaze slid away from mine.

"This reaper has been gathering souls on the mortal side," she said. "And many of them are original believers." I'd been afraid of that.

"They *can* see me then. Why?" I asked.

Naledi frowned as she looked up at me. "I stripped your ability to see a soul's aura. That is what the council requested. No more, no less."

My head felt like it might explode. I gave her a bewildered look. "This isn't a fey game you can wordplay your way out of. If they find out, I'm finished. There's no way Ridwan will let this deceit go a second time."

"If you don't find Vince and retrieve the souls he's harboring, there won't be a second time." Naledi grabbed my hand and squeezed it tight. She swallowed, and her voice dropped to a whisper. "You have the gifts to do the job you're needed for, and you'll continue to possess them until Eternity no longer requires your services."

"Or until the council decides to relieve me of my duties, along with my head." I scoffed and tugged my hand, but she held fast, piercing her dark eyes into mine.

"The remnants of war cannot be so easily swept under the rug. Don't you see?" she pleaded. Her eyes rolled back in her head, the whites showing eerily against her dark complexion. "He waits in the shadows and thinks only of revenge. His opening draws near, and when he strikes, you'll be the only one who can stop him."

I finally managed to yank my hand free and stood up from the couch, stumbling as I put more distance between us. I rubbed my tender wrist and sucked in a few panicked breaths. "Could you please not do that? Ever, *ever* again?" I said, my shoulders shuddering.

Was Vince really so wicked? I mean, he was a scoundrel. No doubt about it. But who the hell did *he* have to take revenge on? And for what? There was also the fact that he'd had a hundred years to make this supposed move. So, why now?

"Sorry." Naledi's eyes returned to normal, and she gave me a pleasant, more neutral expression. "Are you sure you wouldn't like something to drink?"

I stared at her, slack-jawed and furious, and then grabbed my bag and headed for the front door.

"Wait!" Naledi called after me. "I haven't finished giving you the details of your mission."

"Mission? What mission?" I spun around in the foyer, turning back to cut her off at the doorway of the living room. "The Special Ops Unit was voted out by the council."

"Really?" A cunning grin flicked up the corners of her mouth. "So you're meeting up with a fugitive on the mortal side tonight for old times' sake?"

There was no keeping a straight face when it came to arguing with the throne soul. But Naledi didn't see everything. At least, she didn't see enough to be able to whip up a happy ending all the time. Winston's and Josie's deaths were proof enough of that. I wished she had warned me, even if she believed there was nothing I could have done to change the outcome. I would have tried harder. Or maybe I would have burned down Eternity with my efforts. Who knew?

I lifted my chin and glared at Naledi. "No one said I couldn't look for the missing souls on my own time. And now that I'm not captain of Special Ops, it's not my responsibility to bring in criminals like Tasha. That's the Nephilim Guard's job."

Naledi folded her arms. "You're right, but you do have other responsibilities, ones that Khadija wove into your very creation. There is nothing I can do to remove that burden. You must see it through."

I shook my head and migrated closer to the exit. "This isn't some spiritual destiny I'm trying to fulfill. I just want to get the missing souls back—"

"Why?" Naledi asked. "They're not on your docket any longer. Why do you care?"

I ground my teeth and turned away from her. This conversation was not going the way I'd intended. "I want to finish the job I started. I hate feeling incompetent."

"You want to prove that Ridwan was wrong about you."

"Yes." A lump worked its way up my throat, but I swallowed it before adding, "And I want to know what really happened to Saul."

Naledi's silence drew my eyes to her again. The worry in her expression lifted, but not quickly enough.

"You know," I said accusingly. "But how could you? Saul was long dead before you took over the throne."

"There is a collective knowledge that passes from one throne soul to the next," she confessed. Some part of me knew this, from dealing with Winston after he inherited the throne from Khadija, but the strangeness of it was so hard to wrap my mind around.

"So?" I prompted her. "How did Saul die?"

Apprehension seeped through Naledi's features again. "There is too much that lies ahead to concern yourself with the past."

"Well then, by all means, please, tell me what it is I can do for *you*."

She perked, completely overlooking my scathing sarcasm. "Really?"

"No." I choked out an annoyed laugh. "I'm going to track down these souls and make Ridwan eat crow. And then maybe I'll get a straight answer about Saul from Vince."

"I need you to bring those souls to me," Naledi said. She pushed her palms together and shook her hands in a begging gesture. "The council has ordered the Fates to stop sharing soul records with Horus. Now he has no way of knowing when the next original believer will be transferred to this side of the grave. The council also demanded that I remove your ability to see a soul's aura. Don't you see what they're doing? They've ensured that no more original believers join me in the throne realm."

I raked a hand through my curls and then dragged it across my jaw to rest on my chin. "Do they fear a soul uprising?"

"They should." Naledi's voice took on a threatening cadence. "Vince's counterfeit death has helped build and disguise a force far more dangerous than Seth's rebel demons ever dreamed of becoming."

My mouth was suddenly dry. "What are you saying?"

"I'm saying that you need to convince these souls on the other side to join us. Convince them that things have changed—for the better—in Eternity."

"You mean they don't *want* to be rescued?" I thought of Ruth and how she had run away from me. Naledi had come out in the open before the factory souls' disappearance. If Ruth was with Vince, surely he'd heard about it too.

Naledi watched me with a grim expression. "I'm trying to bridge a gap the council has spent over a thousand years creating. Coming into the light was only the first step. I need your help."

My legs felt like they might fall out from under me. "This sounds too much like treason, and I've gotten myself into enough trouble by going against the council's orders."

"The council is going to destroy us all if they keep resisting change. They've forgotten that souls are the very essence that fuels Eternity, and if they continue to drown out the voices of those they depend on, they will only have themselves to blame when the souls rise up and wash over the city in an angry, violent tide," Naledi said.

Her words brought to mind the literal sea of souls that the Witch of Endor had summoned with the Seal of Solomon at the last Oracle Ball. I closed my eyes and shook my head, trying to chase the nightmare vision away. I didn't want to imagine what kind of damage the souls could have done if they'd been coherent and outraged, rather than merely under the witch's zombie spell.

Another upsetting thought rushed in to fill the void. "If Vince is so evil, why did Saul let him live all those years ago?"

Naledi sighed, and her eyes softened with pity. "Poor child," she cooed, reminding me that she was an ancient being, despite the more dominant personality of her youthful, previous life. "He's no more evil than you or I. The answer to your question will only break your heart, and you're going to need that for what's to come."

CHAPTER FIFTEEN

"Hate your job? Join our support group!
It's called EVERYBODY. We meet at the bar."
—Drew Carey

My chat with Naledi was more than I'd bargained for. I'd arrived hoping to find out why certain souls could still see me before leaving their mortal bodies. Instead, I'd left with visions of souls rioting in my head. And, somehow, thanks to Khadija, I was supposed to fix it. Behind the council's back. For free.

If ever I'd had a fuck-my-life moment, this was it.

As per usual, when the world kicked me while I was down, I headed for Purgatory Lounge. My nerves were frayed, and I was supposed to meet up with Tasha in less than two hours. I wondered if the bar in Jamaica had a bartender with an original soul. It was the only perk I could imagine this everlasting death sentence of mine having.

What burned me the most was that the council knew I'd been created as a fail-safe to maintain the Throne of Eternity, and instead of accepting that and applauding my patriotic efforts, they'd condemned and neutered me. They didn't want my help. To them, I was just some lowly reaper, hardly worthy of a pat on the back, let alone any special abilities that might protect Eternity from total disaster. Pride goeth before destruction and all that, I suppose.

The sky over Limbo City was darker when I returned, and a crisp breeze whipped through my hair and drew tears from my eyes. I resisted the urge to dig my wrinkled work robe out of my bag and quickened my pace down Morte Avenue.

Purgatory was lively for a Wednesday night. Not weekend lively, but enough sweaty bodies to create a playful atmosphere. Several off-duty nephilim huddled around a pool table in the back corner, bits of discarded armor scattered on the surrounding tables and chairs. Two female souls watched from the jukebox, their flirty eyes stealing unsubtle glances every so often.

I sat down at a barstool and offered Xaphen the least pathetic smile I could summon when he emerged from the kitchen to greet me. "Heya, kiddo. What can I get ya?" The halo of flames around his crown danced as he grabbed a rag and wiped up a water ring on the bar in front of me.

"How about a mojito?" I said, thinking how nice it would be to enjoy the drink on the beach. Maybe I'd sneak one out and take it to Jamaica with me. I was meeting with a fugitive. What reason did I have to remain professional?

"Make that two of those, and put it on my tab."

I almost fell off my stool when Adrianna Bates sat down beside me. I stammered out a line of surprised gibberish that sounded like I might already be drunk. The nonsensical noise began as a confused question and ended in equally befuddled thanks. I didn't know what else to say.

"Don't mention it," Adrianna replied, a note of humor in her eyes. She shrugged out of her jean jacket and draped it over her chair. Her long, straight hair was pulled back in a low ponytail, and it spilled over her shoulder, almost disappearing against the black turtleneck she wore.

Xaphen turned his back to us and pulled a bottle of rum down from a top shelf before digging a lime and a handful of mint leaves out of the cooler under the counter. He chopped up the lime and muddled it, the mint, and some simple syrup in the bottoms of two rocks glasses before adding in the ice, rum, and club soda.

As soon as he placed the drinks in front of Adrianna and me, the nephilim in the corner cheered. Someone had won their most recent game, and apparently, that meant someone else had to chug a whole pitcher of beer.

"That's my cue," Xaphen said. He filled another pitcher and hurried off, leaving a tense silence in his wake.

Adrianna took a sip of her mojito and cleared her throat. "I should apologize."

"It's okay," I said, feeling my face flush with more heat than her initial insults had generated. "I get it. I'd probably hate me too if I were you."

"That doesn't make it right." She gave me a tight smile and tapped her fingernails against her glass before taking another drink. "Josie was smart. She wouldn't have wasted her time with someone who didn't treat her well. And I know Coreen was in charge of that last mission she went on." She took a deep breath and gulped down some more of her mojito, as if she needed it to get her next words out. "I also realize that your apprenticeship assignment was out of your hands. Saul's too, for that matter," she added under her breath. "I suppose Grim's to blame for that one. He was pissed when Saul stepped down from his position as second-in-command."

My eyebrows shot up in surprise as I sipped at my drink. I was learning all kinds of new things about my mentor this week. Though I did know that, when my generation was introduced, Saul hadn't wanted another apprentice. Grim had assigned me to him anyway. Our relationship started off rocky, but it smoothed out soon enough, and then it had flourished. I'd adored Saul, and I knew he cared a great deal about me, too. What I hadn't known was that he and Adrianna were an item. Apparently, there was a lot I didn't know.

I opened my mouth to say something to that effect, but the ring of my cell phone cut me off, and I ended up apologizing instead.

"Go ahead," Adrianna said, downing the rest of her drink as I answered Bub's call.

"Yes?" I tried to deliver the clipped greeting with a sweet tone, leaving off the pet name I wanted to add since I had an audience.

"Sorry to interrupt your girls' night, pet, but I wanted to check in." He was totally fishing. I wondered if his bug-eyed spy had infiltrated Ellen's apartment and reported my vanishing act.

"Everything's fine," I said, skipping over the detail of my location he was clearly after. "How's the garden coming along?" I asked. Best to change the subject before he could pry any further.

"The white baneberries look a bit shriveled, but I'm hopeful they'll make a comeback."

"And the hounds? Are they behaving?"

"Oh, yes," he said. "Your apprentice left a bit ago. I let his mongrels get a good run in out back."

"You're the best. I'll see you soon. Kiss kiss."

"Kiss kiss," Bub echoed back to me, his words sounding strained as if he weren't quite ready to let me go without getting the answers to his unasked questions.

I hated having to be so dodgy with him, but if he knew where I was, he'd send another fly to tail me. Of that, I was sure. Then the thing would buzz around my face during my meeting with Tasha until I was forced to squash it—forced to squash *Bub,* as he'd so dramatically put it.

Adrianna gave me an amused look as I put away my phone, but she didn't say anything off-color, for which I was grateful. The tabloids had harassed Bub and me enough, and we were finally enjoying a peaceful stretch of privacy, as far as our relationship was concerned anyway.

I polished off my drink and held my glass up to get Xaphen's attention. "I'll get the next round," I said, giving Adrianna a more genuine smile. Maybe my destiny was headed to a figurative hell in a handbasket, but I could forget about that long enough to appreciate her earnest apology. And a few drinks.

After Xaphen replenished us, I tried to recall what I had wanted to say before, and decided instead on, "I miss Saul."

Adrianna nodded sullenly and lifted her glass in silent agreement. She took a long drink and caught an ice cube between her teeth, crunching on it as she stared off into empty space. "I never did forgive him for ending our relationship, among other things. I think that's why he still gets under my skin. It's hard coming to grips with the things you can't change, even after so many years. It's easier to lay the blame on someone else." She paused to give me another repentant look.

"You don't have to keep apologizing. I told you, I get it." I folded my arms over the bar and smiled, enjoying the groveling even as I downplayed it.

She nodded and propped one of her elbows on the bar, turning to angle herself toward me. Over her shoulder, I could see our reflections against the wide front window. The web of flashing red lights that hung from the bar ceiling glittered down on us, dotting our hair and the polished countertop.

"So," Adrianna said, a more relaxed note in her voice, likely the alcohol kicking in. "Asha says you might rejoin the Posy Unit soon."

"Asha speaks?" I snorted. Arden's sailing partner wasn't too thrilled about having to transfer to the Posy Unit after Kevin and I broke off to form the now-defunct Special Ops Unit. Though, honestly, I had a feeling her begrudging attitude had more to do with Arden being in charge than her having to harvest adult souls.

Adrianna chuckled. "She's the strong, silent type, but when she does speak up, you best listen." She took a drink and dipped her tongue into the glass to snag another cube.

"So, have you considered it?" she asked, clinking the ice between her teeth.

I shrugged. "I have an apprentice to think about now. Freelance is a better learning experience. But, damn, if we don't get bumped up to a regular medium-risk schedule soon... Let's just say I'm keeping an open mind."

"The Posy Unit can be educational," Adrianna said defensively. "It's also a great steppingstone to all of the other units, often overlapping with their specialties. The London Beer Flood, for instance. And the Boston Molasses Disaster! Those two could have easily been jobs requiring the Recovery Unit, but I was captain at the time, and the Posy Unit took care of them both."

I grinned. "Point taken."

"And don't tell me you don't ever collect child souls," Adrianna said, pointing a finger at me. "The Mother Goose Unit might be more suave about it, but Arden never would have changed teams if we had the exclusive market on them."

"Fair enough. I'll talk to my apprentice." I'd talk with him about the mating habits of hellcats if Adrianna suggested it. I was just tickled to be having a civil exchange with her. That she had been so close to my mentor touched a tender spot in my heart, too. "I can't believe that Saul never mentioned your romantic connection. Was it some big secret you guys had to keep hidden?"

Adrianna choked on her drink and sat it on the bar as she patted her chest and coughed. Maybe I'd gone too far. The alcohol and goodwill had made me brazen.

"Wow. Really?" She seemed hurt. "He never was the forthcoming kind when it came to matters of the heart, but not a word?"

I gave her a gentle smile and shook my head. "Sorry. If it makes you feel any better, I don't think he told me a lot of things."

Adrianna rolled her tongue over her lips and gave me a thoughtful look. "Saul and I were a century apart. When my generation emerged, I was assigned to Grace Adaline, and Coreen to Saul. Paul Brom was the last reaper to be personally trained by Grim," she added in a hushed whisper, casting a nervous look around the bar as if simply saying his name might get her in trouble.

I kept my mouth shut and waited for her to go on, enthralled by all new details about my mentor. Part of me was angry and hurt at all the secrecy, but another more desperate part of me wanted to know more, *needed* to know more. There was this delusion anchored in my head that if I listened closely enough, maybe I'd hear something that would make sense of all the terrible pieces of the puzzle I hadn't known existed until recently.

Adrianna leaned in closer, her eyes taking in mine intimately, as if she were somehow relieved to be sharing this with someone who had known Saul, too. "I was taken with him right away. This was long before that ridiculous hat and belt buckle, back when he had real style and class." She tsked, but her eyes had gone soft and dreamy. "In the late 1400s, he had this long, leather jerkin that he wore a silver sash over. It made him look like a humble prince. I loved it—but maybe you had to be there," she said, taking in my alarmed face.

"I'm sure it was great," I squeaked, trying not to sound as uncomfortable as I felt. Mentors were the closest thing a reaper had to a parent, and hearing Adrianna get all flustered over Saul's memory was not something I'd expected to have such a reaction to. "Please, go on," I said, trying to force the distaste from my expression.

Adrianna gave me a tight smile as she took another sip of her drink. "Anyway, shortly after my apprenticeship ended, we began seeing each other. And then right before your generation was announced, Saul called it quits."

"Five hundred years?" I whistled.

She nodded sadly. "We fought quite a bit through the latter half of the 1600s, for various reasons. He had all these silly fantasies about us running off together for extended vacations. Like, *extended* vacations." She paused to give me a meaningful look. "He threw a fit when I told him I was planning to take an apprentice. He'd just passed the mantle of second-in-command off to Coreen, and he wanted us to take a month off, now that a new generation had come to lighten our burden."

I thought back to how upset Saul had been at the Oracle Ball that year. It made more sense now. I wondered if Gabriel knew anything about this, and I was anxious to quiz him after our next poker game.

"You know what infuriated me more than anything?" Adrianna said, giving me a strange smile. "Coreen always got first pick when it came time to assign the apprentices." She lifted her hand up to the side of her mouth and whispered, "Because she was sleeping with the boss."

I pressed my lips together, trying to hide my grin. I'd learned that tidbit a while back, but I'd let Adrianna think she was sharing secrets if it would keep her talking.

"Grace usually got second pick," she went on, "especially after she became headmaster at the academy. But she and Coreen both declined to take an apprentice that year."

My stomach clenched, and I bit my tongue, remembering not a second too soon that Craig Hogan had been wiped from existence. So, of course, Adrianna didn't remember Coreen taking him as an apprentice.

She overlooked my uneasiness. "I was next in line, and I chose you." She laughed at my shocked disbelief. "Why are you so surprised? You were at the top of your class," she said.

No, I thought. Craig had been at the top of our class. I had been second. Even if no one else remembered, I did. It almost seemed like I had cheated somehow.

Adrianna's tickled expression slowly dissolved. "So, you can imagine my dismay when you were assigned to Saul, and I was given Vince Hare."

It was my turn to choke on my drink, and I was far less graceful about it. Adrianna slugged me on the back when my hacking didn't subside right away.

"Went down the wrong pipe," I wheezed, deciding it was probably time to get out of there before I slipped up and said something I wasn't supposed to.

How had I not known that Adrianna was Vince's mentor? And did she know that Saul had been sent to take him out?

Did she have any idea that Vince was alive? Did she know what he was up to? I doubted that she did, given how freely she was talking to me.

Adrianna slugged my back again as I hunched over the bar and coughed into the bend of my elbow. "Could we get a glass of water?" she shouted to Xaphen.

"I'm fine," I rasped, waving him off. "Though I would like to get another of these to go. Actually, two," I said, tilting up my glass.

Adrianna gave me a worried look. "You're sure you're okay?"

"Absolutely." I wiped my mouth with the back of my hand and then offered her my other for a shake. "Thanks for the drinks and conversation. It was… enlightening."

"Any time," she said, and I could tell that she meant it.

I paid Xaphen for our second round and my to-go drinks before hooking my bag over my shoulder and shuffling from the bar with my hands full of booze. I looked like a total lush, and after slipping off into a dark alley, it took some serious circus mojo to balance the flimsy plastic cups long enough to work the skeleton coin.

My watch showed that it was a quarter past ten. I didn't expect Tasha for another forty-five minutes, but I wanted to be prepared. Sober? Eh. That was overrated.

CHAPTER SIXTEEN

*"I have never killed a man, but I have
read many obituaries with great pleasure."*
—*Clarence Darrow*

As I caught the skeleton coin on the mortal side, and the Jamaican bar came into view, I sloshed mojito down the front of my shirt and swore.

"Graceful." Tasha was sprawled on a lounge chair near the pool. LED lights filtered through the water, glowing fiercely in the settling dark of night. The glow reached all the way to the surrounding cliffs and reflected off the ocean below, making this nook in the coast look radioactive.

The bar was mostly deserted, with a few employees lingering inside, cleaning up and closing out registers. All the overheads had been turned up, signaling that the party was over, and the light spilled through glass windows, beaming down at the rocky cliffs. Tasha's yacht bobbed against the dock built into the base of the bluff, where a handful of patrons were loading into boats and pushing off. Everyone seemed to be having a good time and getting along. No tragic, unexpected deaths tonight.

"You're early," I said to Tasha, circling the pool.

"So are you. I hope one of those is for me." She sat upright and pulled a loose-knit shawl around her shoulders, knotting it over her bikini top. I offered her a drink, if for nothing else than to free up one of my hands. Then I dropped my bag into an empty lounge chair and touched the wet spot in the center of my shirt. My fingers came away sticky and speckled with mint leaves.

"Super." I groaned, and then slurped at what was left of my mojito before plopping down beside Tasha. "So, what'd you find out?"

"Nothing good." She tucked her legs up, sitting diagonally in her lounge chair. The pool lights touched her face, and I could see the worry lines plaguing her forehead more distinctly now. "I mean, I guess it depends on how you look at it." She worried her bottom lip with her teeth.

"Well?" I set my drink down, deciding I'd probably sucked enough booze into my lungs for one night. It proved to be a smart move.

"Seth is dead."

My initial shock was followed by a lackluster sigh. The guy didn't boil my blood the same way he had back when there was an army at his command. I blinked at Tasha, confused by her distress. Her silence made me wonder if she still adhered to the god's skewed ideals.

"Where's the bad in this?" I asked.

Tasha's aura of concern cracked as she raised a patronizing eyebrow at me. "Who do you suppose offed him, precious?"

Maybe it was the mojitos addling my brain, or perhaps it was all the new and disturbing facts swirling around in there, but I finally caught on. "You think it was Grim?"

"Who else?" Tasha chewed nervously at her lip again. "Also, the way he was found…mutilated and in pieces." She took a shuddering breath. "I don't think Grim's done. That much wrath doesn't get sated in a single kill. Whose blood do you suppose he'll come for next?"

Anyone could have answered that question. Grim made quite the spectacle on the rooftop of Reapers Inc. during the Oracle Ball last year. Seth had been his primary focus, but I'd been a close second. He'd almost taken my head off with his bare hands. Not something I'd forget anytime soon.

A cool breeze whistled across the cliffs and tugged at my hair. I shivered and folded my arms over my chest, even though the night air was warm.

This wasn't what I had come here for. Why was every path I started down lately veering off into the darkest part of the woods?

"What about Vince and the souls?" I asked, looking away from Tasha's concerned gaze.

"Seth's dead, Grim's on the rampage, and all you're worried about are a bunch of misfit souls." She huffed and shook her head. "Well, you're in luck. The news of Seth's gory end has created mass hysteria, and Vince's hoard of souls is playing musical lairs. Everyone's gathering tomorrow night at a new sanctuary. They're abandoning their current home base for fear it's been compromised."

"So, these souls are actually following Vince? Like he's some kind of cult leader?" I hadn't wanted to believe Naledi, but it was hard not to now.

Tasha shrugged. "Look, I don't know what they've got going on. I've only been stuck on this side for a few months, and I've been enjoying the beach far too much to get myself tangled up in another lost cause."

"Then how are you getting all this information? How are your demon contacts in the know? Are they working with Vince, too?"

"No demons," she said. "I talked to a few souls."

My skepticism went into overdrive. "Why would they talk to *you*?"

"Look at me." Tasha nodded down at her carefree ensemble. "Do I look like a reaper to you?"

"You mean they think you're a soul?"

She nodded and stretched her legs out on the lounge chair before leaning back on her elbows. "Why not? I'm not parading around in a black robe, so that definitely helps."

"I guess so," I said, trying to relax in my own chair, but I was too on edge to make it look as casual as Tasha did. My boots squeaked against the white plastic, leaving scuff marks behind. Tasha took me in with a teasing air about her before going on.

"One of the souls I bumped into actually tried to recruit me, but it was the second one that gave up the goods," she said with a sneaky smile. "Their numbers are impressive, and even though they have a headquarters of sorts, they don't all live there together. It's not a commune or anything like that.

All I had to do was ask the guy if I'd seen him before, if he knew Vince."

"That really worked?"

"Like a charm." She looked awfully proud of herself. "It's amazing what a boy will spill if you only smile pretty and bat your lashes. He asked if I'd gotten the notice about the shindig, and then went on about Seth—" Her good humor dwindled at the mention of the god, and she turned her frightened eyes up at me. "You really should watch your back, Lana."

"I gathered that much." I rolled my eyes. If only she knew how much I'd had to do that over the past two years.

"I'm serious." Tasha sat up again, kicking her feet over the side of her chair and resting her mojito on her knee so she could face me squarely. "The things I heard… I know we're not the best of friends, but you helped me out when you didn't have to. The least I can do in return is give you a proper warning."

I blew out a long breath. "What am I going to do? Run off and hide out on a beach somewhere until this all blows over?"

"Works for me," she said in a whispered singsong before reclining in her chair again.

"Well, I can't." I felt my mouth stretch into a miserable line. "So why don't you tell me about this lair everyone's meeting Vince at tomorrow?"

Tasha barked out a laugh. "Do you really want to walk in on that? You know he's been collecting these souls for, like, a century now. And they actually seem to *like* him. If he's brainwashing them, he's doing one hell of a job of it. No matter how you slice this shit pie, going into that den spells suicide."

I gritted my teeth. "Naledi's prepared to offer them asylum in the throne realm for now. Vince... I don't know what I'm supposed to do about him, but since damn near everyone else thinks he's dead, I guess it doesn't really matter if I off him in the process of getting these souls back."

Tasha made a face at me. "They're souls. A dime a dozen. Why do you care so much about what happens to them?"

A million replies grasped for the tip of my tongue. *Because these aren't just any souls. They're super souls! Because I'm the chosen one. Because I'm a pouty brat, who wants to do the good thing and then stick her tongue out at the asshat who doubted me. Because I'm dying inside not knowing the truth about the man who molded me into who I am.*

I pushed those answers away and settled for, "Why *don't* you care what happens to them?"

"Excuse me?" Tasha looked at me like I'd grown a third eye.

"This is what we were made for. Our whole purpose is wrapped up in the fate of souls, in getting them where they belong. Can you really tell me that you don't care at all? Not even a little?"

"Jesus Christ," Tasha groaned. "You really are a goody two shoes. And here everyone thought you were such a slacker."

I felt my cheeks grow hot. "And everyone thought you were a heartless wench, but you stuck your neck out for Tack, a junkie demon who ditched you after you saved his ass." Her face twisted at the reminder, and I tried to backpedal before I lost any more ground. "My point is, people change. Even reapers. We're evolving into better versions of ourselves all the time."

"Pretty sure the best version of me is on a deserted beach with an endless supply of these." She slurped at her mojito before looking at me with a thoughtful frown. "Are you sure you're not the one who's brainwashed? I mean, you were special order, precious. You sure that's not having some effect on your better judgment here?"

My brows drew together, and I turned to glare at her. I hated her pet name for me, but more than that, I didn't care for the insinuation that I was playing the part of a puppet.

It wasn't that the thought hadn't crossed my mind—I'd been the throne soul's girl Friday ever since Maalik introduced me to Khadija. Sometimes, I was able to trade off that feeling for the illusion of a noble knight. Like I was the right hand of the regal ruler of some secret society. Eternity's last hope. The Obi-Wan of the afterlife. Lately, I just felt like everyone's bitch. Always being ordered to fetch this or that soul—more so than my day job required anyway.

"It's not the weight of being a psychopomp alone that motivates me," I said, turning my head to look at Tasha. "My mentor was sent to terminate Vince. Now, he's dead, but Vince is still alive. I want to know what happened."

It was true, I realized. More than anything else, I wanted to know what had really become of Saul. Rubbing lost souls in Ridwan's face wouldn't restore the Special Ops Unit. Hell, it might not earn me an apology, or even a thank you.

Tasha's eyes glittered in time with the lights dancing across the surface of the pool. Stretched out on the lounge chairs with our mojitos, we looked like a couple of girlfriends on vacation. I closed my eyes, trying to imagine the sun shining down on us. A life of exile in the mortal world didn't seem so bad right now.

"I can't get involved," Tasha said suddenly. "You get that, right?"

"I'm not asking you to fight my battles. I just need you to point me in the right direction."

She sighed and sipped at the melting ice at the bottom of her cup. "The soul who filled me in is supposed to be meeting me in Atlanta tomorrow night. He said the venue is hard to find in the city, but I'm pretty sure he thinks this is a date." She smirked and gave me an accusing look as if to say she was enduring this for my sake. "Meet me at the Oakland Cemetery around seven-thirty. The souls avoid it for fear a reaper will spot them. You can tail me from a safe distance, but as soon as we get to Vince's hiding spot, I'm gone, and you're on your own."

"Deal," I said, my stomach tightening into a sour knot as I realized I'd have to bail on the make-up night I'd promised Bub. Shit. Why did villains always have to throw a wrench in my date nights?

I hated to admit it, but this had been the easy part of the mission. Now I had to somehow come up with a plan to convince all the souls to come with me to the throne realm. But first, I wanted to corner Vince and ask him my questions about Saul. Getting him to talk would be no easy feat, but I had a few cards up my sleeve.

Tasha's suggestion that the souls liked Vince made me revisit Naledi's words. *He waits in the shadows and thinks only of revenge. His opening draws near, and when he strikes, you'll be the only one who can stop him.*

So maybe she wasn't talking about Vince. After all, he hadn't tried to kill me the last time I saw him. My attempt to comfort myself backfired instantly as I realized that only left Grim, now that Seth was dead. I was fairly certain Naledi hadn't been talking about me fending off that particular strike. Tasha's warning to watch my back suddenly felt like very good advice indeed.

First things first, I thought. Vince was a weaker mark, with a significantly smaller grudge against me, and I had some idea of how to find him now. Best to start there and leave the impossible for later.

CHAPTER SEVENTEEN

*"Even if I knew that tomorrow the world would go to pieces,
I would still plant my apple tree."*
—*Martin Luther*

It was after midnight before I made it home, and when I went upstairs to change, I was surprised that Bub wasn't asleep. The hounds had already migrated from the doggie bed to ours, their backs pressed up against the footboard, more than likely hoping to go unnoticed. They took up a good quarter of the mattress, and while Bub would complain, I knew that he enjoyed tucking his feet under their warmth as much as I did.

I quickly changed out of my work clothes and stepped into the adjoining bathroom to wipe a washcloth over my neck and chest where sticky mojito had dried to my skin. Then I pulled on a pair of shorts and a tank top. The lacey fabric smelled like brimstone, and I made a mental note to ask Bub to stop hanging my clothes outside to dry. Maybe in a few days. Definitely *not* tonight. That certainly wasn't the best way to start the conversation we needed to have.

As I headed downstairs, I glanced out the wide window that connected the dining and living rooms and spotted a lantern hanging out in the garden. Bub was hunched over beneath it, his hands working the earth vigorously. A pond on the opposite side of the lantern post rippled as something broke the surface. I hesitated at the French doors, peering through the dark to get a better look.

"There you are." Bub stood and wiped his hands down the front of his jeans. His bare chest made my breath catch, sweat glittering across taut muscles in the lantern light. He pushed back his disheveled hair, leaving a smear of mud over one eyebrow.

"You've been busy," I said, ignoring the irritation in his tone. My eyes flicked over to the pond, and I decided to sit down on the patio stairs instead of venturing into the garden.

Bub frowned as he made his way over to me. "Did you have fun with Ellen?" he asked, a sharp edge to his voice as if he were daring me to lie.

"I did." I nodded slowly. "Then I enjoyed a few drinks with Adrianna Bates at Purgatory Lounge. You can call Xaphen to verify that if you'd like."

Bub's eyes narrowed. "That's where you were when I called, I take it?"

"Did your spy not inform you?" I snorted. "There goes his Christmas bonus."

"Hilarious." Bub sat down on the patio steps beside me and leaned in for a kiss. His lips were salty, and the amount of mud coating his boots told me he'd been hard at it for some time.

"What's with the pond?" I asked, trying to postpone the uglier part of our conversation to come.

"Do you like it?" Bub's mouth drew up in a lopsided smile. "I wanted to add a few water plants, and I… I—" He paused to give me a tense smile. "I adopted a pet octopus."

"What?" My head jerked up, and I glanced out over the garden again to the pool.

"I stopped in at Hades' Hound House to grab some more Cerberus Chow, and she was all alone in a tank near the register, with the saddest button eyes," Bub said sweetly. "Wait till you see her. She's gorgeous."

"What's she eat? How big is she going to get?" I asked, folding my arms with a frown. I decided not to wonder aloud if this was such a good idea when Bub released a disheartened sigh.

"She eats crabs and clams mostly, which are easy enough to come by, and she's not one of the larger varieties, so she shouldn't get too big. We're not talking about Cthulhu here."

"What are you going to name her?" I asked next, trying not to sound so annoyed.

Bub perked again, giving me one of his more charming smiles. "Ursula."

"Okay, then." I chuckled and wiped a dried smear of dirt from his shoulder. Bub caught my hand as I pulled away.

"So, are you going to tell me where you went after the bar?"

The question caught me off guard. I'd thought he was content to drop the matter, but apparently not. At least he didn't sound jealous, which led me to believe he had some idea of what this line of questioning would reveal.

"I met with Tasha on the mortal side," I said, my gaze slowly pulling up to meet his. "I know where Vince Hare and the missing souls are. And I'm going to get them back."

"Lana." Bub sighed and squeezed my hand, dragging it down to rest on his knee. "This is dangerous, and no one is asking you to do it."

I pressed my lips together and pulled my hand away, tucking it between my legs with my other one. This suddenly felt like a bad idea, but I'd already made up my mind to be forthright with him, so I pressed on.

"Naledi asked me to do it. If someone doesn't put an end to Vince's cult on the mortal side, the next war will be instigated by souls rather than displaced deities and demons."

Bub ran both hands over his head and then rested his arms on his knees. "What does the council think of all this? I thought they did away with the Special Ops Unit."

"How do you know that?" I gawked at him. "I only just found out this morning."

"Asmodeus." Bub gave me a humorless smile. "He's been summoned to fill the void I left on the Hell Committee, and he's none too tickled about it. Cindy told him, and he called to tell me. I told you I don't send my foot soldiers into the Reapers Inc. building," he added as though he thought I hadn't believed him when he told me before. Then his eyebrows lifted, prompting me to answer his original question.

"The council doesn't know what I'm up to. They've been doing everything in their power to stop Naledi from adding more original believers to her growing brood. They don't trust her."

"But you do?"

I nodded. "I may not always care for her methods, but she sees what's coming, and she does what she can to keep the peace in Eternity."

Bub reached for my hand again, pulling me closer to him on the patio steps. He wrapped his arm around my shoulders and pressed his forehead to mine. "Promise me you're not doing all of this to churn up the past."

Not for the first time, I got the feeling that Bub knew more than he was telling about Saul's death. The thought gnawed at me, especially when he ordered his minions to buzz all up in my business any time they caught me speaking to someone about my late mentor. Maybe what he knew painted Saul in an unflattering light, and he didn't want to tarnish my memories. Or perhaps he was afraid that I'd follow his pointed finger down a vengeful path of no return.

I searched Bub's golden eyes, his face a mere inch from mine, and tried to read the thoughts beyond his gaze.

"Promise me," he begged again, his voice dropping to a sultry whisper.

"Only if you promise that you're not keeping the truth from me."

Bub's eyes closed, and he pulled away abruptly. "Bloody hell. You're never going to let this go, are you?"

"You *are* hiding something. Why?" I huffed and shook my head with disbelief. "If you're so worried about me putting myself in danger to discover the truth, why not tell me what you know?"

"Because nothing good can come of it," Bub shouted.

The outburst made me flinch, and I recoiled when he reached for me again. Bub groaned miserably. The sound encompassed the full spectrum of defeat. He rubbed his hands across the tops of his thighs, brushing away crumbled dirt from his jeans.

My heart pumped more eagerly, waiting for his next words, and a lump pushed its way up to the back of my throat.

"I told you that I suspected Vince was alive. Remember?"

I swallowed and nodded. "You said there wasn't any proof, though."

"Just a short-lived rumor, love." Bub's face pinched with regret. "Saul had already disappeared. He was gone for nearly a week when someone on the council suggested that he was trading on the ghost market. After all, he'd been assigned a high-risk harvest the last day he reported for duty, and the soul was never recovered."

I shook my head, refusing to believe it, but I bit my tongue to keep from interrupting Bub.

"The very next day, Grim announced that Saul's mutilated body had been found. That he'd been the victim of a brutal demon attack on the mortal side. A statue was erected, and the rest is history."

"That was a rumor," I snapped, clinging to my denial. "You said it yourself."

"Yes." Bub glanced down at my hand as if he wanted to retake it, but he refrained. "It *was* a rumor. But now that we know Vince is alive—after Saul reported the reaper's death…" He let the accusation hang in the air while I continued to shake my head.

"Maybe he thought he'd killed Vince and was simply mistaken. That's possible, right?"

"It's also possible that Grim sent someone to terminate Saul before he could incite any other reapers into joining his cause."

"Then why put up a statue in his honor? Why go through the trouble of sugarcoating it all?" I gave up the head shaking and hugged myself, struggling to come to terms with everything.

"Think about it," Bub said. "Reapers stepping out of line made Grim look weak. He'd already had to deal with Vince Hare. But a second one in such a short span of time? The council would have come down hard on him. They might have even prevented him from introducing new generations. It's been suggested before."

I thought of Miranda Giles, the reaper Grim had pulled out of existence right in front of me. No one remembered her insubordination—well, except Grim and me. I wondered if that was the idea. How many other bad little reapers had been wiped from existence and conveniently forgotten for the sake of political gain?

"So Grim called Saul a hero," I said, filling in the blanks. "And he put up a fancy statue to hide the fact that he'd lost control of another of his minions." My shoulders trembled, and I hugged myself tighter, feeling broken inside.

Bub took his chances and reached out for me again. I let him this time, sinking into his embrace as tears crept into my eyes. "You don't have to remember him that way. There's no real proof. Vince being alive could very well be an honest mistake, like you suggested. And no one else has reported a sighting in over a hundred years. All you have to do is let this go."

"Nice try." I sniffled against his shoulder. "Not liking the facts doesn't negate them, and there's still Naledi's warning to consider. If the council ignores it, I'm Eternity's last defense."

"My gallant death merchant." Bub rubbed his hands up and down my back and kissed the top of my head. "You smell like a Caribbean bar."

I chuckled softly and reached up to wipe a tear from under my eye. "The meeting with Tasha was BYOB in Jamaica."

"I'm filthy, starving, and knackered," he murmured into my hair as if to say he didn't want to talk about my questionable activities anymore. "Shall we take a bath?"

I nodded and took his hand as he stood, letting him pull me to my feet as well. A bubbling noise in the garden caught my attention, and I glanced over in time to spy the set of button eyes that had clearly captured Bub's heart earlier in the day. A single tentacle broke the surface of the water, almost as if she were waving goodnight.

Bub clucked his tongue. "Brilliant, no?" He grinned and smacked his free hand over his jeans again, dusting off the remaining clods of dirt before we stepped through the French doors.

I wasn't sold on the idea of having a pet octopus, but maybe she'd grow on me. Though hopefully not in the literal sense. In fact, I was pretty sure I could do without her sticky little suckers coming anywhere near me.

Bub didn't mind the hounds. He fed them and kept an eye on them whenever I didn't require their help at work. But it seemed like it was more out of obligation than adoration. To be fair, they had been gifted to me by an ex-lover. I could understand his reservations.

If Ursula had been a gift from the rebel succubus Bub had pretended to woo while undercover, I'd probably have reservations, too. But she wasn't, and for that reason alone, I decided to suck it up and do my best to accept her into our strange little family.

Bub's gaze fell on the hounds as we entered our bedroom, and he made a displeased noise under his breath. Saul had wiggled his way up to the center of the bed. He'd be getting the boot after our bath. Bub ignored the slight for now, choosing instead to scrounge around in the dark for some clean boxer briefs, while I stripped out of my shorts and tank top.

After we'd closed ourselves in the bathroom, I lit a pair of candles, and Bub filled the clawfoot tub. It was too late, and we were both entirely too tired to get frisky, but the quality time together was nice, even if fleeting. I still hadn't told him that our date night would have to be rescheduled, and I wasn't looking forward to it. Maybe that could wait for the morning. I didn't want to spoil what was left of our time together.

A dark thought clouded the back of my mind, but I pushed it away until we were tucked in our bed, with Saul and Coreen banished to their doggie bed in the corner.

What if things didn't end well tomorrow? What if Vince chose fight over flight this time? What if his horde of souls decided to launch their long-awaited war by putting my head on a pike and invading Limbo City?

For all my doubt-mongering, I found room in my head to continue questioning Saul's death. Maybe he had been a traitor like Vince. Worse yet, maybe he was the one who recruited Vince. He'd been Grim's second-in-command for centuries, a position that earned him an inside look at the boss man's most corrupt secrets. Coreen had known about Khadija when she had the position, and Saul had filled that spot for centuries before she had. He must have known.

I couldn't deny that vengeance was motivating me as well. Saul was a good man, a kind man—traitor or not. He'd never wronged me. On the contrary, he'd taught me everything I knew about soul harvesting. And he had shared his home and his boat with me. That alone was enough motivation to crucify whoever had taken him out of my world.

Vince, Grim, a random minion—I didn't care. Someone had an unpaid bill, and it was time to collect.

CHAPTER EIGHTEEN

"The life of the dead is placed in the memory of the living."
—*Marcus Tullius Cicero*

A nephilim gardener was raking leaves out of the flowerbeds surrounding the memorial statues when I arrived at the park after work Thursday evening. The task seemed pointless, as the tulip trees were still shedding, an endless shower of golden confetti raining down on the bright green lawn. It was a sad reminder of my own never-ending job.

I gripped my cup of cider and held it up under my nose, savoring the warmth in the chilly breeze. My other hand pinched together the open folds of my leather jacket. I hadn't thought to zip it up while I waited in line at Nessa's donut shop, and after walking a couple of blocks through the city, I was now certain that a witch's tits had nothing on mine.

I hastened my steps through the memorial park and set my cider down on Josie's bench. Jack-o-Lanterns had been placed on either side of it. They watched me with toothy grins as I zipped up my jacket over the white blouse I'd worn to work. It had been a gift from Ellen, and while it wasn't really my speed, I'd chosen it with Tasha in mind. She'd said that the souls considered her one of their own, likely due to her lack of a black robe and more human attire.

I sat down and rubbed my hands together before taking up my cider again. It was the perfect temperature for a day like this. I took a sip and smiled at the name engraved in the marble bench.

"Hey, lady," I said softly, knowing full well that Josie couldn't hear me. It wouldn't stop me from speaking to her. "Sure wish you were around to talk me out of this stupid thing I'm about to do."

I kept finding myself here lately, pining over Josie and fretting over Saul. Neither of them could be replaced. No one even came close. I'd spent a fair amount of time with Ellen, Adrianna, and Tasha the day before—granted, the last two on that list probably didn't consider me girlfriend material. It was discouraging. I hadn't exactly been trying to *replace* Josie, but while I didn't need a mentor anymore, I did long for friendship.

I sighed and checked my watch before taking another drink of cider. My meeting with Tasha was in an hour, but I had agreed to meet with Bub half an hour before that on the ship. Our morning chat about canceling date night had taken an unexpected turn, though I wasn't too surprised. Bub was coming with me to confront Vince. I'd resisted his backup offer until he started quoting John Wayne at me. *A man's got to do what a man's got to do.*

I wasn't stupid. I knew bringing him along was a good idea—and I knew that he'd come anyway even if I refused his help. I just hoped he didn't try to interfere when I started questioning Vince about Saul. Because I *would* be questioning him.

My priorities had been evaluated enough, and I was sure of them. Souls to Naledi first, vengeance second—unless an irresistible opportunity presented itself, for example, Vince confessing to Saul's murder, and his head being right there for the taking. That seemed like a reasonable excuse to go off script to me.

"Greetings, my dear," Warren said as he dropped out of the sky, landing in the small clearing between me and the memorial statues.

"Do you have it?" I asked before his wings had folded against his back.

Warren held up a wooden box, then paused to wipe the corner of it off on the front of his blue, mechanic jumpsuit. "Eight souls. *Eight*," he repeated with stern eyes.

"Cross my heart." I reached for the box with my free hand and cradled it in my lap. "You're the best. I owe you big time."

"The device isn't approved by the council for widespread use yet," Warren said, scratching his cheek thoughtfully. "And the details you shared about this trial run were a bit fuzzy."

I nodded. "I know, I know. These factory souls want to remain anonymous though, so I really can't share more than I have." It wasn't an outright lie. *Ruth* certainly wanted to remain anonymous.

I wasn't sure how useful the soul gauntlet would be yet, but I had a few ideas. Maybe I'd pretend to lead the rogue souls into battle and then dump them in the throne realm.

Surprise! You can all just hang out here until you learn to play nice, mmkay? Naledi and her Apparition Agency probably wouldn't find that tactic too amusing, especially if the hoard of souls destroyed their realm in a massive tantrum. But, technically, I could call that mission accomplished, right?

Warren shrugged at my vague explanation. "So long as you share your data. I can't perfect this tool if I don't have legitimate test results to work with."

"Absolutely. First thing in the morning," I said.

"Good. I better get back to the shop. New recruits for the Nephilim Guard are in need of weaponry." He waved as he took flight, ascending through the golden boughs of the tulip trees. I returned the gesture and watched him go, stifling a laugh when he nearly collided with a ghostly stork on its way to the factory.

When my gaze dropped, Maalik was standing before Saul's memorial. He faced away from me, his silver wings and folded hands resting against his back. A stab of panic urged me to leave before he turned around, but common sense reasoned that it was too late.

"Some say that concealing the truth is not the same thing as lying." It almost sounded as if he were talking to himself. He turned around, giving me the full burden of his stare. "I suppose you and I have that belief in common. Though I do it for the sake of peace. I'm not sure what excuses you tell yourself."

"What do you mean?" I asked, folding my arms over the box Warren had delivered.

Maalik closed the distance between us and sat on the opposite end of Josie's bench. His wings fluttered up over the back of the white marble and settled again, their tips dragging the ground below. This close, I was able to get a good look at him. His black robe was free of wrinkles, and his mane of dark curls was sleek and shiny. He looked better than I'd seen him look for some time, despite the cynicism warping his features.

"Where's Tasha Henry?"

My eyes bulged at the seemingly random question. "How should I know?"

Maalik's jaw flexed and the beginnings of hellfire swirled in his eyes. He meant to intimidate me into a confession. "You were seen at her last known location by one of the guards on watch duty, and without a soul on your docket to use as an alibi. Would you like to try again?"

I mirrored his nasty look. "What? A girl can't enjoy an island getaway without needing an excuse now?" I pushed past the impulse to crack another joke, seeing as how he was unmoved by my scapegoat humor. "I was looking for Tasha, okay?" *Didn't get more truthful than that.* "I thought finding her might help me keep the Special Ops Unit online," I added for good measure.

That truth was somewhat sketchier, but in a roundabout way, it was fact. I'd found Tasha, and she was leading me to Vince and the missing souls, which might have kept the Special Ops Unit going if it hadn't already been shut down.

Maalik looked unconvinced, though the smoke swirling in his eyes dissipated. "What's in the box?"

Panic coiled around my heart again, and my hand gripped the box tighter. "What's with the twenty questions?" I asked, taking a careful drink of my cider. It had been meant to look casual, but I was afraid my shaking hand ruined the ruse.

Maalik sighed and rested an arm across the top of the bench. "Naledi asked me to accompany you tonight."

"What?" I gasped and almost fell as I scrambled off the bench and got to my feet. My cider sloshed onto the grass, and I clutched the box to my chest. "Then why are you badgering me with all this cloak and dagger bullshit? You ass!"

I expected Maalik to look pleased with himself as if he'd just played some grand joke on me. The prank of the century. But, instead, anger and doubt clung to his aura.

"I do not like volunteering my aid to those I cannot trust," he said. "Maybe you're not lying, but you're certainly not sharing all the details."

"Why should I?" I snapped. "Tell me. Why should I share anything, after seeing the way the council reacts to truth? They wanted to *kill* me, Maalik. And you were going to let them!"

He winced at the accusation. "I did everything in my power to stop it, and when I realized I couldn't, I had to trust that Naledi would sort things out." His eyes were moist when he turned them up to meet mine. "Even if she hadn't, I would have done something, *anything*, to stop them from harming you."

I wanted to believe him, but we'd been trading carefully disguised lies for too long now. I willed the sadness heaving in my chest not to reach my eyes. My throat tightened, and I had to swallow a few times before I was able to speak again.

"I don't need your aid, voluntary or otherwise," I said through clenched teeth.

"You can't go after Vince alone tonight. That's reckless—"

"I never said I was going alone."

Maalik pulled in a sharp breath through his nose. "The council does not trust the Lord of the Flies—"

"And I don't trust the council. So, I guess we're even," I said, not caring how petty I sounded. "In any case, this isn't official council business. Or didn't Naledi tell you?"

His eyes smoldered again, stoking the fires of my own wrath at the same time. "Naledi involved me. I'm council, so it is council business now, and I say the Lord of the Flies cannot be trusted."

I scoffed, barking out a loud, clipped laugh saturated with spite. "I trust Beelzebub more than anyone, and that includes you." He jerked at the insult, as if I'd slapped him. "If he doesn't come tonight, neither do I."

"He is spawned from evil. It is his nature to deceive and spread lies—"

"As far as I can tell, he's the only one being honest with me. A hundred years, and no one else has bothered to tell me the truth about Vince or Saul—"

Maalik's chest heaved, and his eyes blinked fiercely. "How did he find out?" He glanced past me over to the statue of my mentor. It took me a moment to recognize the look for what it was. Guilt.

"You," I whispered, dropping my cup of cider and the wooden box. "It was you?"

The world spun as Maalik's tormented gaze met mine. Any remaining doubt was washed away in a wave of fresh misery. The realization that he'd given himself up was painted all over his face.

"It was a long time ago," he choked out, stumbling over the words as he watched me. "I didn't know you. It was an order. And Saul had become a legitimate threat."

I felt a familiar rush of heat spread down my arms. If I hadn't been so furious, I might have been alarmed.

No more, no less. Naledi had said.

If I'd wanted to, I could have taken three steps across the park and sunk my hands through his chest. I could have pulled the concentrated soul matter that made up his essence inside out, letting it disperse into the darkening sky.

I wanted to. I wanted to so badly that it hurt to look at him.

I'd shared a bed with this man. He'd had the nerve to tell me that he loved me, knowing that he'd killed my mentor. The comment about concealing the truth not being the same thing as lying struck my heart like an uppercut.

Maalik's gaze ripped away from mine and dropped down to my hands sticking out from the cuffs of my leather sleeves. His eyes widened, and I was sure he could see my wrath building beneath the surface.

"Stay away from me," I said softly, the demand laced with an unspoken threat.

I reached down to scoop up the wooden box and my empty cider cup before stalking out of the memorial garden. Before I reached the park entrance, I ducked behind a row of hedges and flipped the skeleton coin, taking it to the throne realm.

Naledi had some explaining to do.

CHAPTER NINETEEN

*"If we have no peace, it is because we have forgotten
that we belong to each other."*
—Mother Teresa

The sky was brighter in the throne realm. It stung my eyes as I marched up the front steps of the cottage.

"Naledi!" I pounded on the front door. The hinges of the wooden box creaked under my arm, complaining about my vice-grip hold.

Father Ron greeted me with a startled expression. "Ms. Harvey. Is everything all right?"

"No. Where's Naledi?" I asked, pushing past him and inside the cottage foyer.

"This really isn't a good time," he stammered before following me around the corner and into the living room. "We're in the middle of a meeting."

A dozen faces turned to stare at me. Even without my special soul vision, I could feel the weight of their auras filling the small space. They didn't appear to have much else in common, with their varying races and cultural attire. A few were older, but most looked to be somewhere in the gray range of midlife.

Naledi stood at the center of the mass, wearing her burlap dress. It managed to look even more regal as she drew everyone's attention. "For those of you who do not know, this is Lana Harvey, the reaper responsible for our newfound status in Eternity," she said, announcing me as if my visit had been expected. Knowing her, it very well might have been.

The souls clapped enthusiastically, flashing broad smiles and exuding genuine gratitude. I recognized Morgan, the youngest of those present, at one end of a sofa. She sat next to a familiar soul I couldn't name, but I remembered him watching me with wary eyes through a window the day before. All traces of suspicion had vanished now that I'd been properly introduced.

"We need to talk," I said to Naledi, curbing my tone as much as I could, considering the duress I was under.

"Of course," she cooed. "Our meeting was just adjourning."

The souls stood up on cue and filed past me, some pausing to shake my hand or murmur some blessing or another. I felt my face warm with the compliments. Naledi followed them to the door, and I followed her, watching as she waved them off, and they meandered back to their old-world homes built into the neighboring hills.

As soon as Naledi closed the front door of the cottage, the dam holding back my inner turmoil ruptured. "I know Maalik killed Saul, and there's no way he's coming with me tonight."

Her smooth features showed no surprise, and I hated not knowing how much she actually knew. She clasped her hands together under her breasts and gave me a neutral expression. "I understand your objection—"

"No buts," I said, narrowing my eyes. "There is nothing you can say to change that. I don't care how all-knowing you think you are. Either I do this my way, or you can send Maalik out to chase his tail. I somehow doubt Tasha will be interested in working with someone from the council who ordered her execution."

"Okay," Naledi said. "We'll do this your way."

I waited, expecting her to say something more to convince me otherwise. When she didn't, I turned away from her and dragged my hands down my face. "How could you even think that was a good idea? He *killed* my mentor."

There was a fight brewing in me, left over from Maalik's accidental confession, and not even Naledi's compliant mood could pacify that. I paced the foyer like a caged beast, waiting for something to justify unleashing my wrath.

"I know," Naledi said. "I've always known." *Well, that would do.*

"Are you fucking serious? How could you keep that from me?" I screamed at her.

"Why should I have told you?" she asked, opening her hands gently. "What would you have done? Killed a member of the Afterlife Council?"

I growled up at the vaulted ceiling, and my rage echoed back to me. "Did you know that I would find out this way when you asked Maalik to accompany me tonight?"

"I did," Naledi confessed in her annoyingly passive voice. It made it hard to come out of the gates on her without feeling like Jerk of the Year. Through my mounting anger, I stumbled over reason.

"You were counting on it. Weren't you?" I gave her a wide-eyed glare.

Naledi nodded. "I can't trust you to convince these souls to come home if you're hell-bent on revenge. Now that you know the truth, you can focus on what's important."

I coughed to muffle the sob creeping up my throat and unzipped my jacket. It was suddenly way too hot, and I couldn't suck in enough air. "Saul was important. He deserves to be avenged, and now that I know I can't do that, you think I'm the best person to preach peace and forgiveness to an assembly of disgruntled souls? Are you nuts?"

Naledi smiled softly, a twinge of amusement shifting her features. "I know you are. And I hope you'll remember that Maalik was following orders when your mentor met his end."

I ground my teeth at the reminder. "There's no love lost between me and the council, but Maalik was the one to snuff out Saul's life. I can never forgive him for that. I might have to let him live, but I don't ever want to see or speak to him again."

"I understand," Naledi said. She crossed the room slowly, pausing before the hanging incense burner in the corner. Her fingers traced the edges of the golden plate, and the first stirrings of anger burned in her eyes. "Trust me, I understand."

"That's easy for you to say." I huffed. "You ripped the Witch of Endor's heart out after she killed Winston."

Naledi frowned at me. "It didn't bring him back to me. And Seth was equally to blame, yet he walked free."

"Not for long."

Her eyes blinked in surprise, and I couldn't help but grin.

"He's dead. Tasha found out from a few souls and demon contacts on the mortal side. Apparently, it was a grisly affair." I enjoyed her shock a moment longer before adding, "Wow, you really can't see everything. Huh?"

She raised an eyebrow. "I never said I could. Being all-knowing is such a fluid label." She shrugged and then nodded at the box under my arm. "That will not serve you well. The souls gathered on the mortal side are many."

I shrugged. "So, I'll have to make a few trips."

Naledi didn't look confident in my plan. She opened her mouth as if to say so, when a scream from outside had both of us spinning toward the front door. I jerked it open before she could protest.

A rift split the ceiling of the realm in half. Black night rolled off into the east, and a white, cloudless sky spread to the west. Where the divide cracked open, a thin sheet of rain cut over the land, forming a muddy river as it gathered in the low ground between the knolls.

The scream came again, cutting off in a guttural, inhuman wail halfway through. My hand went to my throat automatically as my mind guessed at the sort of violence that could cause such a noise.

I took a shaky step down the front porch of the cottage, and Naledi's hand clamped over my shoulder.

"Wait," she hissed.

A body smacked the ground in front of me, not two feet away, and I yelped in surprise. Limbs splayed every which way. The outfit was fresh enough in my memory to deduce that this was the soul who had been sitting next to Morgan. As I stepped in to get a closer look, I noticed the soul was missing its head.

Naledi made a mournful noise in the back of her throat. "We're too late," she whispered, her fingers digging deeper into my shoulder.

"Naledi!" Morgan called out as she ran across the lawn toward the cottage. Her small hands were covered in blood, and her pupils were dilated with terror. "Father Ron is dead," she sobbed. "What's happening?"

Something flapped in the sky overhead, casting a shadow over the sunny half of the lawn. I took a timid step out from under cover of the porch and looked up, feeling the breath squeeze from my lungs.

Grim hovered in the sky. The black wings he had once kept tucked beneath his flesh to disguise his Greek origins fanned behind him, and corded muscles encased his naked body. The sight of him was made even more alarming by the soulish head held in his hands. Grim's eyes filled with black, and the sky crackled with energy as his hands began to glow. They melted through the soul's skull, and then Grim pulled outward, stretching the soul matter like a Chinese finger trap until it popped.

Soul matter exploded in the air like fireworks, but instead of watching it dissipate, Grim leaned into it. He took a long, heaving breath, shuddering as the soul matter entered his mouth and nose. He seemed to expand with it, like a balloon filling with more air. When he was done, his black gaze slowly dropped to mine, taking me in as his head cocked to one side.

I couldn't breathe. I tried to swallow, but my mouth was too dry. Naledi tugged at my arm, but I was only vaguely aware of it. I couldn't take my eyes off Grim. I was too afraid he'd eat me alive if I did.

A sob from below broke Grim's attention, and only then did I feel safe enough looking away. Morgan had fallen to her knees. She held her bloodied hands out in front of her, staring at them helplessly. My heart reeled as Grim twisted in the air and then darted for her.

"Hold this." I shoved the wooden box into Naledi's arms and ran across the lawn, digging the skeleton coin from my pocket.

As I neared Morgan, I threw myself on top of her. The coin was already in the air. Grim's furious face descended on us, and his hand grasped out. I had a moment of uncertainty. What would happen if he caught the coin before I did? What would happen if he smacked it out of my reach? It was all I could do not to close my eyes and curl into the fetal position.

Time seemed to slow as the skeleton coin fell toward my open palm, and when my fingers finally closed around it, I still couldn't breathe. Not until we reappeared in front of the cottage and snagged Naledi.

I gave Grim one last look, too terrified to manage a victorious sneer, and then I flipped the coin again, taking me, Naledi, and Morgan to safety.

CHAPTER TWENTY

"**W**e have to go back." Naledi turned wide, agitated circles on the beach at the edge of the Sea of Avalon. The isle of the fey that Morgan hailed from had risen above the water in the distance. Torches sparkled along the shore, outlining its perimeter against the dark sky, and wild music carried across the sea, bringing with it a trio of small canoes.

Una, the faerie queen who adored Morgan, stood in the center boat, her red curls glittering with strange treasures—some of them living—and the white dress she wore glowed softly with a light all its own. It spilled out across the water, helping the fey oarsmen stay on course.

Morgan sat in the wet sand, awaiting their arrival. The red tights she wore were torn, and tears streamed down her face. She hadn't said two words since we left the throne realm.

"We have to go back," Naledi hissed again, her hands wrapping around my arm frantically. The box that contained Winston's soul gauntlet lay abandoned in the sand.

"They're all dead," Morgan whispered. The crickets singing in the evergreens that bordered the shore on either side seemed to quiet with her declaration. "It happened so fast. I'd forgotten my book, and Father Ron stopped by to return it. When he went to leave—" She heaved out a quivering sob. "That monster snatched him up. I was so frightened. I ran to Allister's cottage, but all I found was blood sprayed across his lawn. That's when I ran to Naledi's."

"We have to go back," Naledi said, yanking at the sleeve of my jacket more urgently.

"Don't you see?" Morgan shrieked at her. "We're all that's left. All that stands in his way. He means to take the throne for himself."

"He can't do that," I said, looking from Morgan to Naledi. "That's impossible, right?"

Naledi let go of my arm and sighed. She dropped onto the sand beside Morgan and pulled the girl into her lap. "The structure of Eternity is evolving, whether the council wills it or not."

I hated when she spoke in riddles, nonsense that sounded vaguely ominous or hopeful. It did nothing for me. At least, nothing good. Anger bubbled inside me again, and I felt the pressure and heat layering itself behind my heart.

"What's that supposed to mean?" I shouted and held my head with both hands, trying to make sense of it all. An awful feeling of dread swirled in my gut, and I swayed on my feet.

Naledi's eyes found mine, and I felt grounded again. For the moment.

"Listen carefully," she said as she stroked Morgan's hair. "The throne can be given and it can be taken. It's as simple as that. The rituals and teas are pretense, built up in an elaborate shroud of mystery meant to discourage others from attempting a takeover. An original believer's soul matter is more concentrated, more potent. It's true, we are best suited to rule a world that is funded by our kind. But what Grim's doing, consuming that power rather than letting it flow back into the fabric of Eternity…" Her breath caught and she paused to swallow. "Morgan is right. If he finds us—if he finds *me*—he is powerful enough to take the throne."

"No, no, no," I chanted, shaking my head as I turned away from her. I stumbled a few feet away and fell to my knees, retching in the tall grass behind the beach.

"Lana?" Naledi whispered through the dark, as if she were afraid to be left alone.

I laughed, unable to bridle my hysteria. Grim had ripped open the sky of the throne realm and slaughtered a dozen of the most powerful souls in existence. And that was before he consumed their essence and got all supercharged. There was no way I'd look like anything other than a bug in need of squashing to him.

The imagery made me think of Bub, oddly enough, and I glanced down at my watch. I was supposed to meet him at the ship ten minutes ago.

"My sweet fawn!" Una called out as the three canoes scraped bottom and came to shore. She stayed in the boat but reached her hands out eagerly.

Morgan pulled away from Naledi and threw herself into the queen's arms. "Oh, Una!" she sobbed. "It's terrible. All the souls in the hidden realm are dead. Thanatos is loose and on the march. Lana was only able to save Naledi and me."

Una's severe brow turned solemn. "All of them?" She lifted Morgan off the beach and placed her in the boat. Then she turned to me. "Little Death, do you recall the boon you swore to me?"

The faerie queen had granted Bub and me overnight asylum last year, after I'd rescued him from the rebels, and before his name had been cleared by the council. All it had cost me was a rain-checked promise I was sure I'd live to regret.

I sucked in a tense breath and nodded. "I do."

Una lifted her chin and held my gaze. "Never return to this place, and you can consider it fulfilled." Her eyes swirled with warring emotions. I could see that she was grateful, but I could also tell that she blamed me for the danger Morgan had endured. I'd collected her from the isle in the first place, and now I was returning her in an unacceptable condition. Una was warning me that should I ever try to take her sweet fawn again, she would find some way to make my life hell. The boon she'd pardoned would be forfeit, and I'd pay with blood next.

"Naledi?" Morgan gave Una a pleading look.

"The throne soul is wanted by a vengeful god. We cannot endanger our people by inviting her onto the isle. You understand, don't you?" Una ran her delicate fingers down Morgan's cheek and under her chin. The girl shuddered and her eyes blinked as if she were coming out from under a spell. A peaceful look softened her features.

"Dearest, Naledi," Morgan said, turning her attention to us. "She is right. You are hunted by Grim Thanatos, and there is nothing I can offer to aid you. I am so sorry." Tears welled in her eyes again, but her defeat was plain. I couldn't ask any more of her. Even as an ancient soul, I saw her innocence. It was the same way Una saw her.

Naledi stood and folded her sand-crusted hands over her heart. "Be well, Morgan. Perhaps we will meet again when this darkness is behind us."

Una's unnerving stare shifted to the throne soul, and I could tell she wanted to issue another threat, but she had nothing left to bargain with. "We take our leave across the sea," she said, nodding to the fey oarsmen in her boat. They pushed off from the shore and began rowing toward the isle in the distance. The drums played faster, and excited voices rang out, welcoming Morgan home.

Naledi watched with lonely eyes. "The fey hold her in such high esteem. They consider her even more sacred than the Christians count their saints or Horus his favored pharaohs. She is a special soul, reigning over a world that conforms to neither side of the grave. I had hoped to learn more from her before our time together came to an end."

I followed her gaze across the sea and rubbed the goosebumps crawling up my arms. "She doesn't seem to be doing much reigning to me."

"That's the beauty of it," Naledi said. "She is the heart of that world, but she does not inflict her rule on any being. They have their own governing forces, but they come together where protecting the one who dreamed them into existence is concerned. They don't fear or mistrust her. They don't bicker over her for political nonsense."

"Speaking of political nonsense," I said. "Where am I supposed to bring the souls Vince is harboring, provided I'm able to coax them over to this side, now that the throne realm is compromised? And while I'm asking that question, how the hell did Grim do that?"

Tears brimmed Naledi's eyes, and an overall sense of hopelessness emanated from her. "It's my fault," she said softly. "Applying a sunlight schedule to the throne realm created a window of opportunity, weakened seams at daybreak and nightfall."

"Can it be fixed?" I asked.

Naledi looked up hopefully. "Yes, I think so."

"Then do it." I glanced down at my watch. If I didn't leave now, Tasha would think I'd bailed on her. There was no time to meet Bub at the ship. I dug my phone out of my pocket and pressed it into Naledi's hand. "Call Beelzebub, Gabriel, Kevin—anyone else you trust—before returning to the throne realm. Don't take any chances. Grim could still be there."

Naledi caught my arm before I could turn away. "Be careful, Lana. Vince has many original believers. They are dangerous enough on their own, but if Grim is looking to gain more power, their gathering would be an ideal target."

The thought had occurred to me. "I know," I said, swallowing hard. That wasn't something I needed to worry about right now. Not if I didn't want to lose my nerve.

I bent down to pick up the wooden box out of the sand and opened the lid, revealing the new and improved soul gauntlet Warren had crafted. The dials had been upgraded to steel. I pushed up the jacket sleeve of my left arm, and a soft, insulated liner brushed my skin as I clasped the silver cuff onto my wrist, right over a patch of faint, rippled scars left by my first test run.

If all else failed, the joking plan I'd proposed of making several trips back and forth would work in a pinch. And this was definitely a pinch. The bruising, rip your flesh off kind—especially if I got stupid and overworked the gauntlet again.

If I had a chance to use it in the first place.

CHAPTER TWENTY-ONE

"The idea is to die young as late as possible."
—*Ashley Montagu*

I hurried through Oakland Cemetery, rushing past monuments and stumbling over grave markers in the fading daylight. Dewy grass clung to my boots, and the smell of rotting grave flowers filled my nostrils. Lightning lit up the clouds in the dark sky, and they grumbled, threatening more storms to come.

The plot of land the cemetery occupied was nearly fifty acres. I'd agreed to meet Tasha in the historical section in the southwest corner—which left six acres to comb through. I suddenly wished I'd thought to request a more specific rendezvous point. My nerves were too shot to be wandering around in a graveyard at night with Grim on the prowl. I was almost crippled by relief—and a killer Charlie horse—when I finally spotted Tasha.

"You're late," she said, looking down at me from where she reclined on an elaborate monument—two feminine, concrete figures sitting beneath a cross. Tasha's legs lay over their laps, her arms looped casually around one's neck. She'd traded her beachwear for a pair of jeans and a ragged, black pullover sweater, making her look more like the displaced rebel I remembered from the streets of Limbo City.

I hesitated, wondering if my excuse for being tardy would scare her out of following through with her favor. I didn't have to wonder for long. She jumped down from the monument and made a face as she touched a finger to my cheek.

"Is that *blood*?"

I took a deep breath and gave her a tense smile. "If there is a fan, the shit just obliterated it."

"Just be glad Daddy didn't come home and take the paddle to you." Tasha hiccupped out a short laugh. When she realized I wasn't laughing with her, the humor quickly melted from her face. The whites of her eyes seemed to glow in the dark, pooling around the shrinking rings of her irises. "You're fucked. I shouldn't be anywhere near you."

"Tasha!" I grabbed her arm as she turned to leave. "Please. Take me to Vince's lair, and I'll never bother you again."

Her eyes roamed the cemetery as if she expected Grim to jump out at any moment and grab us. It made the hairs on my arms stand at attention. I didn't think there was any way Grim could track me. Of course, I hadn't thought he could tear his way through the throne realm sky either.

Tasha's breath grew labored, and her arm shook in my grasp. "I can't, Lana. I'm sorry."

"Then at least tell me where you're supposed to be meeting this soul. I'll follow *him* instead."

"There's a coffee bar on the other side of Memorial Drive," Tasha whispered. She reached her free hand up and ran it over her face, tucking her knuckles against her chin. Her eyes hadn't stopped their frantic searching through the dark, and she wouldn't look at me. "The soul has a beard, and he was wearing a green beanie the last time I saw him. His name's David."

I let her arm go, and she stumbled back a step. I expected her to hurl some catty remark at me, or at least give me a dirty look for her lost footing, but she just reached up and yanked the hood of her sweater over her head.

"Be careful, precious," she said. For the first time, there was no hint of ridicule in the nickname. A gleaming coin appeared in her hand, and then she vanished, leaving me alone in the cemetery as it began to sprinkle.

Atlanta was a big city, and I was familiar enough with it from my harvests that I knew the coffee bar Tasha had mentioned. It was just south of my current location. I wound my way through the tombstones and mausoleums until I reached the short brick wall that bordered the cemetery. I followed it to the entrance that opened onto Memorial Drive. A chill settled in my bones as the sprinkle advanced to a full-on rain. I grasped the shoulders of my leather jacket and pulled it up, holding it over my head as I ran across the street to the sidewalk on the opposite side.

A few patrons wielding umbrellas ran past me and into a restaurant advertising catfish and beer. They didn't notice me, as expected. I slipped around the building to the side street that led to the coffee bar. The handful of trees spaced down the brick sidewalk didn't provide much shelter from the rain, but I pulled my jacket down and zipped it anyway, deciding

I'd rather have soaked hair than look like I'd just won a wet tee shirt contest.

I slowed down as I neared the coffee bar and tried to think of a better plan. There wasn't much in the way of decent cover besides a full parking lot, but something told me that lurking around cars in the rain wouldn't look especially casual while I staked out the place. The rain complicated things in more ways than one.

Lost souls, as they were called even if they happened to be runaways, were a strange breed. Staying on the mortal side for too long could have adverse effects. They had to be handled carefully, which was why there was a whole unit dedicated to the process. I was grossly underqualified, but Craig Hogan—my reaper-turned-rebel and then unexisted ex—had been on the unit, and I had helped him study. So, I knew a thing or two. Which was to say, I knew enough to know this could go horribly wrong.

A lost soul who was newly deceased *might* experience the elements on the mortal side. It was possible that I'd find Tasha's unsuspecting date dripping wet. He sounded like quite the newbie. But if he'd been around a while, maybe even as little as six months, there was a chance the elements wouldn't affect him. He *might* be completely dry. And then there were the lost souls that got all uppity about either being dead or being stuck on the mortal side. They were what the humans sometimes called poltergeists. The elements didn't matter with them. They *were* the elements. The Lost Souls Unit had special shackles and chains for harvesting that sort. Unfortunately, I didn't have any on hand.

The only thing I did have going for me was the fact that I wasn't wearing my work robe. Tasha had said the souls considered her one of their own without it. All I was hoping for was to go unnoticed. As long as this David fellow didn't see anyone walk through me while I stalked him, maybe I'd get lucky.

I reached the coffee shop and wandered past the front window with my hands casually stuffed into the pockets of my jacket. Out of the corner of my eye, I checked out the customers inside. The water-spotted glass made it hard to discern the hazy opacity of a soul—a very slight difference that distinguished them from the living—but no one wore a green hat, and the only beard I saw was a scraggly white thing that belonged to an older gentleman. That seemed like a detail Tasha wouldn't have left off, so I dismissed him and circled the parking lot beside the establishment. When I passed by the window for a second look, not much had changed. At least, not inside. Out in the rain, my teeth had begun to chatter, and my drenched, unfurled curls stuck to my face.

This would have been significantly easier if Tasha had hung around long enough to give me a few more details. Like maybe *when* she was supposed to meet up with this soul. How long had she intended to hassle me in the cemetery before this date of hers?

I groaned and walked across the street, hoping I'd be less conspicuous there. Then I spotted a Victorian house sitting up on a hill catty-corner from the coffee bar. It had a wraparound porch curtained by a dozen hanging plants, but beyond those, I noticed a rocking chair. And it was dry. No one would complain if I watched from there, seeing as how the humans couldn't see me. Another rumble of thunder followed by a crack of lightning finalized the plan.

I hurried down to the end of the block and crossed the street. The concrete stairs leading up to the house were slick with moss and lacked a railing, so I had to tread carefully in the downpour. Rainwater saturated the lawn, and small streams raced past me on their way to the street below, spewing forth from the house's gutters. When I finally ducked under the roof of the porch, my shoulders dropped down from their hunched position near my ears, and I released a breath I hadn't realized I was holding.

I peeled off my jacket and spread it out over the porch swing, giving it a chance to dry out. My white blouse stuck to my skin, and I almost stripped out of it too, before remembering that the soul I was waiting for would be able to see me just fine. I grumbled under my breath and settled for pinching the bottom hem and fanning the fabric to get a little airflow between it and my skin. I soon gave up on that task and opted to squeeze the dripping water from my hair instead.

The rain hushed to a light patter, and I peeked through the gangly vines framing my view of the coffee shop while I preened, watching for any sign of my mark. From the higher ground, I could see the edge of the Oakland Cemetery farther up the street. A few spotlights surrounding the more notable monuments had flickered on, including the streetlights running along Memorial Drive, and two city workers were locking up the front gates for the night.

As the minutes slipped by, I began to worry. What was I going to do if he didn't show? What if Grim had gotten to him and the rest of Vince's souls first? How I wished Bub was here with me. If only one of his flies had tagged along today, but I was sure he hadn't thought it necessary, since I was supposed to be meeting up with him at the ship. I wondered if Naledi had been able to reach him, at least.

I paced the porch, more out of agitation than in hopes of speeding my dry time. It seemed a little pointless since I'd have to go right back out in the rain to follow David—if he ever showed up—and knowing my luck, that would be when the sky decided to cut loose again.

Water had found its way under the soul gauntlet on my wrist, soaking through the liner and making it feel like steel wool against my skin. I dug a fingernail underneath it, absently scratching as I watched the coffee shop. Now that my mind didn't have an immediate task and I was forced to pause, thoughts began to assimilate.

Maalik had killed Saul. Maalik had *killed* Saul.

And there was nothing I could do about it. My blood pumped fresh, hot wrath. Even though it had happened before my relationship with the angel, even though that relationship was long over, it was hard not to feel betrayed. Had he really thought I would never find out? The deceit wounded me so completely that I was still reeling from it.

When Grim made his surprise appearance, the jolt of shock and survival instincts had filled the forefront of my mind. But now that had worn off, and my wrathful intent spilled over onto Grim, too. After all, he'd given Maalik the order to kill Saul. If I could do nothing to extract retribution from Maalik, Grim would have to take the full burden.

A flash of green hat caught my attention, and my eyes focused as I shook off my murderous daydream. A bearded man—a soul, from the ashen tint of his skin—sat down at one of the tables on the abandoned patio outside the coffee shop. The sprinkle of rain wasn't so severe that he looked mental for hanging out in it, but the way he nervously glanced around told me this was Tasha's guy.

His gaze roamed the area surrounding the coffee shop, and as it reached up the hill toward the Victorian house, I ducked behind one of the posts holding up the porch roof. I bit my lip, hoping I'd moved out of sight in time. I counted to ten and then dared a quick glance down the hill again.

He was gone. *Shit.*

I grabbed my jacket off the swing and hurried down the porch steps, my boots squishing as they hit the lawn. From here, I could see everything. I searched the parking lot and the streets, branching off in all directions and cluttered with more cars. A few customers wandered out of the coffee shop, laughing as they walked arm in arm around the corner. The noise turned the head of a man farther up on the opposite sidewalk.

He'd lost the hat, and I might not have noticed him if he hadn't turned around, but the beard gave him away. Unfortunately, my rash decision to spring out into the open lawn gave *me* away. David's eyes flashed with recognition, and he bolted, tearing down the sidewalk toward the cemetery.

I skipped the steps and slid haphazardly down the steep lawn. When I reached the street, I chased after him, yanking my jacket on as I went. The storm clouds had moved on, and night had settled over the city, giving me only a glimpse of David as he passed under the streetlight at the corner. He turned east down Memorial Drive.

My lungs burned as I willed my legs to run faster. With all the manor construction and randomness of life, Bub and I had gotten lazy with our desert mountain runs, opting instead to watch the hounds from the comfort of the patio. I was kicking myself for that tonight as my breath rasped and wheezed past my lips.

When I reached the corner, I paused to rest my hands on my knees and glanced down the street. David was almost two blocks ahead of me, his ashen consistency blending into his surroundings the farther away he got.

"Screw this," I hissed, digging the skeleton coin out of my pocket. I flipped it in the air and rode the current between this world and the next. It deposited me behind the short brick wall at the far corner of the cemetery, a couple of blocks up in the direction David was headed. I could finish catching my breath while I waited for him. The streetlights stretched down the opposite side of the avenue, the side David was on, but they didn't touch the shadow where I lurked, so I was able to sneak glances over the wall.

Tasha had said she'd passed off as a soul without her robe, but I didn't see how that was possible with the way David had reacted to me. I could understand Ruth's reasons now since she knew me personally. But was my face so recognizable to souls on this side?

When David reached the corner across the way from me, he shot a quick glance over his shoulder. A frustrated crease touched his brow, and he slowed his pace as he tugged his green hat back over his head. Then he crossed the street.

I held my breath, resisting the urge to jump over the wall and tackle him. It would have been so gratifying. But then I'd have to torture the information I needed out of the soul, which wouldn't be nearly as fast as just following him. So I rotated against the inside corner of the cemetery wall and continued poking my head up to catch glimpses of his green hat as he rounded the corner and headed up the sidewalk.

The wall was taller where it curled northward, shifting from brick to rock. But the street on this side was darker too, with not as many streetlights, and lots of full trees casting shadows. I grabbed a low branch and used it to pull myself up on top of the wall where I trailed David from above.

When he cut across the street and headed for Cabbagetown, I hopped down off the wall and ducked behind a cluster of shrubs, watching him through a thin spot in the foliage. He glanced over his shoulder again, and a small grin pulled at his mouth as his transparency began to increase. The wrought iron fence along the sidewalk was suddenly visible *through* him. He turned sharply and stepped right past it, going solid again before taking off across a parking lot stretched out before several apartment buildings.

Definitely *not* something a newbie lost soul should have been able to pull off. Vince was training them. The realization was alarming, even though it made perfect sense. He couldn't have his disgruntled souls getting picked off before he had a chance to charge them into battle. Especially if he expected them to wait around for a hundred years.

I fetched my skeleton coin again and flipped it to get past the fence. Maybe I didn't have all the proper training to collect lost souls, but I had my own bag of tricks. I ran after David, my boots slapping against the asphalt as we gave up our pretense. I followed him to a chain-link fence on the far side of the parking lot. He used his ghostly fading trick again, but I was faster with my coin this time, appearing on the other side as he solidified.

"Ha!" I shouted, too excited to have won the chase to care that he hadn't taken me all the way to his destination. He'd clearly known that I was following him, so there was a chance that he was leading me on a wild hunt.

David lifted his hands and gave me a sheepish grin. "You got me."

"Where are Vince and the other souls?" I demanded.

"Who?" He blinked at me with mocking innocence.

"See this?" I pulled up the sleeve of my jacket and tapped a finger on the soul gauntlet. "I can suck your soul into it with the press of a button."

His eyes lit up sarcastically. "Fancy. The Ghostbusters should be calling you."

"Okay, smartass. You asked for it." I launched forward, thrusting out the gauntlet.

Concern flickered through David's expression, but I only had a split second to wonder if it was genuine or mockery.

Something heavy cracked against the back of my skull, and a metallic echo vibrated in my ears. I fumbled forward, my outstretched hands slipping past David as I collided with the pavement.

The streetlights distorted my vision as I rolled onto my back, and muddled voices swarmed around me. It sounded like I was underwater. *Sleeping with the fishes so soon?*

The edges of my sight began to darken, but not before a silhouette towered over me, and then Ruth Summerdale's face blurred in and out of focus.

"I should've taken you to Hell," I slurred, my head lolling limply between my shoulders.

The pain shooting through my skull finally subsided, taking my consciousness with it.

CHAPTER TWENTY-TWO

"It is true that I have had heartache and tragedy in my life.
These are things none of us avoids.
Suffering is the price of being alive."
—*Judy Collins*

I woke with a migraine and a bitter taste in my mouth as if I'd bitten my tongue at some point between my failed attempt to grab David and being dragged off to... *Where the hell was I?*

I squinted around the dark room. Rope cut into my wrists as I struggled to sit upright, and a metal pole pressed against my spine. My hands had been bound around it behind me, and I realized that the soul gauntlet was missing. Great. Warren was going to kill me. If I made it out of here alive anyway.

A muffled chorus of voices cheered somewhere in the distance, and I strained to listen as someone spoke over them, rallying them into an even louder, roaring crescendo. I couldn't make out any words. It was all angry gibberish that sounded vaguely like a call to action. Definitely not what Eternity needed right now. This had to be stopped, and fast.

I yanked at the ropes around my wrists, but they were tight, and the metal pole had no interest whatsoever in budging. I pulled in my legs, drawing my knees up to my chest, and then shimmied against the pole as I stood, mindful of my aching head. The pride from completing the action didn't last long, considering this was as far as I'd be going. In addition to the gauntlet, I was also missing the knife I kept in my boot. And after a bit of wriggling and writhing, I concluded that the skeleton coin was gone, too.

A slice of fluorescent light cut across my face as a door opened. I was momentarily blinded. Then a lamp clicked on in the corner, and I could see a vague outline of the room. It sort of looked like an office in a warehouse. It was dusty and mostly empty, but that didn't mean there wasn't an active operation here. Lots of warehouse offices looked like this one. I'd harvested enough factory souls to know. Unless a human had special sight, they wouldn't notice a bunch of squatter souls hanging around while they worked.

They wouldn't notice me tied up in their office either, I thought, scowling as my eyes adjusted and Vince Hare came into focus. Ruth sat on a desk behind him, wearing *my* fucking jacket. The lamp sat on a corner of the desk too, and it wobbled as she folded her legs and gripped the edge of the desk with both hands.

"Lana Harvey," Vince said, stopping in front of me. "I was expecting Tasha, but this is even better." He'd been wearing a standard-issue black robe when I'd bumped into him at the hospital, but tonight he was in a pair of jeans and a black, long-sleeved tee shirt. He held the end of his braided hair in one hand and the hunting knife I kept in my boot in his other, flicking it across his hair as if trimming split ends.

"Nice, isn't it?" I quipped. "The hellcat I castrated with it thought so, too."

Vince sniffed and gave me an amused grin. "Such grit. I suppose you came by it honestly, being mentored by Saul Avelo."

I pressed my lips together and turned my face away from him, choosing to glare at Ruth instead. "I should have sent you straight to Hell when I had the chance."

Ruth scoffed. "You said that earlier." She tapped a finger against her temple. "But maybe I rattled your brainpan too much for you to remember."

"I remember," I snapped. "I just wanted to make sure you did, too."

"Honey, I spent damn near a century in a *factory*. It doesn't get much closer to Hell than that." She jumped down off the desk and walked over to stand beside Vince.

"That's my jacket," I said, having nothing wittier to come back with.

"Oh?" Ruth lifted an eyebrow and gave me a snide grin. "Is this yours, too?" She stuffed her hand down into one of the jacket's pockets and pulled out the soul gauntlet. Then she dropped it on the concrete floor and brought her boot heel down on it, busting the domed cap and snapping the hinges that joined the two cuff pieces together.

I thought of Warren again and groaned.

Vince made a face at the mangled device. "You kids and your fancy technology. Back when I was a reaper, we had to use bribery and threats to gather our souls," he said in a joking curmudgeon voice while waving a fist in the air.

"You're *still* a reaper," I reminded him. "Just because you dropped off the grid, doesn't change what you are."

Vince sighed and pinched his lips together, giving me a jaded nod. "Maybe so. But Saul taught me to go big or go home—"

"Saul was *my* mentor, you prick!"

"Ooh, touchy subject." He recoiled and pretended to shudder in fright. "You're right. Saul *was* your mentor. And then you started kissing *derrière* to move on up in the world—or to Paris, anyhow—while I stayed behind in the States and helped Saul clean up all the Manifest Destiny carnage." He shrugged at my surprised horror. "Guess that's why he passed the torch to me instead of you."

"What torch? There's no fucking torch. What you're doing is treason, plain and simple." Bile burned at the back of my throat, and I took a shuddering breath before swallowing to keep it down. The pain in my head was growing, but I wasn't sure if it was due to Ruth trying to brain me earlier, or if it was because I couldn't handle what Vince was suggesting.

He looked at me for a long moment, pity filling his eyes. "Eternity needs reformation. It's needed it for a good long while now. Saul knew that. The souls created that world, and they deserve to have their say in how it's run. They deserve more freedom and better choices—"

Ruth huffed. "Because having to choose between working in a factory for a century or being dumped in a mindless sea is bullshit."

"Sorry, *honey*, but not all dogs go to Heaven." I rolled my eyes.

Ruth sucked in an offended breath, but Vince edged in front of her when she tried to come at me. "Saul started this movement," he said, giving her a warning look before picking up where he'd left off. "My cover was blown before his, and he helped fake my death so I could do more for the cause on the mortal side."

"And where's *she* come into all this?" I asked, eyeing Ruth over his shoulder. "She's just a plain old factory soul."

Vince grinned at my jab, seeing that I was enjoying getting under Ruth's skin. "Every good resistance needs an inside man—or woman," he added, glancing back at Ruth. "When Saul's soul on the inside was about to retire from the factory, he recruited her for us. She made the choice to leave and join the Army of Souls before her own retirement, giving up the luxury of being born into a celebrity family on this side."

I balked at the confession and unwillingly lost some of my grudge against the girl. "You'd rather live as a ghost on this side, with no one able to hear or see you?"

Ruth's gaze met Vince's briefly, and a coy smile turned up her lips. "I'm heard and seen well enough." *Ah, love.* Even the crazies couldn't escape Cupid's arrow.

"So, what's the plan? Gonna storm Limbo City and form a picket line in front of Reapers Inc.? Demand shorter factory terms? Insist on a new afterlife for nonbelievers who didn't earn a ticket to Heaven?"

"You're smarter than that, Lana." Vince smirked. "We have half a dozen original believers in our midst. The souls are beyond the point of asking or demanding. It's time to take what's rightfully theirs."

Ruth wrapped an arm around his neck and leaned in closer to me as if she were sharing gossip between friends.

"We're going to seize the Throne of Eternity and fix everything wrong with the afterlives."

"Good luck with that." I leaned back against the pole and shook my head. "I can't believe Naledi wanted to offer you asylum in the throne realm."

"Naledi is a puppet of the enemy," Ruth said, a hoity bite to her voice. "She wasn't chosen by the souls. She was chosen by the council—"

"Actually, she was chosen by *me*." That got both of their attentions.

"But the papers—the press conference," Ruth stammered, her gaze jerking from me to Vince.

"They wanted everyone to think they chose Naledi, to believe they were still in control of the situation. But I found her on the mortal side, and I brought her to the throne realm, and she assumed the throne long before any of them even knew there was a throne to assume." Okay, that wasn't entirely true. Horus and Maalik had known about the throne. I suspected some of the other council members had an idea too, but they'd kept their mouths shut for the sake of peace.

"Why you?" Vince asked, pointing the hunting knife at me with a thoughtful look as if he'd forgotten what he was holding in his hand. "You've been all over the papers these past few years, for everything from dating a council member to launching a rescue mission through Hell to shutting down the ghost market." He paused to give me a scolding frown. "Something I'm still upset with you over, by the way. I was one of their top bidders."

"Of course you were." I snorted. "And I'll bet the souls were so grateful when you bought them from their demon captors, never once thinking that they wouldn't have gone through all that in the first place if assholes like you didn't keep funding the horrible practice."

The point of my hunting knife looked less casual as it neared my face. "I was *one* of their top bidders. Not their *only* bidder. All of the souls downstairs would be in someone else's possession if not for me, and I can guarantee that those someones had far less honorable intentions."

"Whatever," I said, trying to keep the panic out of my voice as I leaned away from the knife. "You're no better than the rebels."

Ruth shook her head. "The rebels wanted to destroy Eternity. We want to fix it."

"And how exactly do you plan to do that?" I snapped. "*Seizing the throne* is a pretty vague plan. Did it take you the whole century to come up with that one?"

Her expression turned malicious again. "Don't forget that you're the one who's tied up, honey."

"Look," I said, trying to restrain the swell of clashing emotions flooding through me. "You need to come with me to the throne realm and talk to Naledi. Work all of this out with her, where it's safe."

My heart tightened as I remembered the rip through the throne realm sky and the blood on Morgan's hands. But Naledi had said she could fix it. I was hoping she could also fix this mess with Vince and his Army of Souls. She *had* requested that I bring them to her. I hoped this was still a good idea. I didn't want to be the idiot on the field who scored the winning goal for the other team.

Vince circled me, tapping the tip of my knife against his shoulder. "You *want* to bring us to the throne realm, do you?"

"No. Absolutely not," Ruth said, her eyes widening at him as if he'd lost his mind. "We can't trust her to lead us there. It's obviously a trap orchestrated by the council."

"Please. Naledi sent me, not the council. They have no idea I'm here. They don't even know that Seth's dead yet, or that Grim's hunting down original believers and consuming their souls so he can make a grab for the throne himself." I wanted to enjoy the rise I was getting out of them, but the truth scared the shit out of me too much for gloating. "That's right," I said. "Your half a dozen fancy souls are in big danger."

Ruth and Vince edged away from me, moving closer to the desk so that they could share a private moment. They stared at each other, guarded expressions tightening their faces. Whatever silent language they were speaking was lost on me. My head hurt. My shoulders hurt. And I was freezing without my jacket. That would be the first thing I fixed when we got to the throne realm. The bitch would be returning my jacket, and Vince would be giving my knife back. If this went on for too much longer, I was going to add interest in the form of black eyes for both of them.

"Come on, guys." I groaned and yanked at the rope around my wrists again. "I wouldn't have bothered coming here at all if it wasn't so important. Naledi wants to unite forces or bridge gaps, some crap like that. Grim needs to be stopped, and the original believers need to be protected. We can at least agree on that much, can't we?"

A sad look passed through Ruth's eyes as if Vince had given her the wrong answer, even though he hadn't said anything I could hear or understand. "A hundred years," she said, a hand pressing over her heart. "I've been faithful to this mission. To *you*. And you want to throw it all away?"

"Ruth." Vince set my knife down on the desk and took both of her shoulders in his hands. "This mission is supposed to end in peace. If there is a way to achieve that without violence, don't you think we should take it?"

Angry tears filled her eyes as she turned them on me again. "You really trust her that much?"

Vince snorted out a soft laugh. "Saul was her mentor. That tells me all I need to know. Besides," he added, turning to look at me, "if she betrays us, I'll gut her with her own knife."

"Can't wait," I said dryly. "Now, would someone please—"

A scream from outside the office cut me off, freezing my heart in my chest. Another scream followed, and then a whole chorus of nightmares rang in my ears as Vince opened the door. He and Ruth ran from the room. I wanted to shout after them to stop. To come back. That it was too late.

But I couldn't get the words out. I could hardly draw in my next breath.

Vince had left the door ajar, and the deafening sound of Death hard at work filled my ears, rattling me to the core. My legs slid out from under me, and the metal pole at my back pressed achingly into my spine as I slumped to the floor.

I pushed my cheek against my shoulder, wishing my hands were free to hide my face in, and sobbed silently as I waited for my turn to come.

CHAPTER TWENTY-THREE

*"The dead cannot cry out for justice.
It is a duty of the living to do so for them."*
—Lois McMaster Bujold

The screams of those dying downstairs in the warehouse couldn't have lasted more than a few minutes. But I swear it felt like an eternity. Their raw, ethereal swan songs ricocheted through my skull, tearing at my mind. When they tapered off, panic flooded in. My limbs shook with fear as silence settled around me, and my breath grew shallow as I listened for footsteps, for flapping wings.

I sat there like that, in trembling comatose, long enough that my muscles cramped. Cold air seeped through the crack in the door, and I began to blame it for my shaking, dismissing it as a violent case of the shivers. I had to clench my teeth to keep them from chattering.

With my final moments lurking dangerously close, my thoughts slipped off into the past, and Saul entered my mind. Why would he have done this? What did he have to gain from starting a soul rebellion? What did Vince have to gain?

Ruth seemed like a clue in and of herself. Had Saul had a soulish lover later in life, too? I thought of Adrianna and all she had said about him. She claimed her ambitions had been what ended their relationship. Had that been what crippled my friendship with Saul, too? There were no concrete answers. I felt like I had a million more questions than I'd begun with. *And now I'd never have the answers*, I thought, as something scraped across the floor of the warehouse, echoing a warning that reached up to me in the office.

I bit my lip and willed my breath to steady and be silent. A thread of hope that Grim wouldn't find me had crept into my mind, and I wasn't ready to give it up just yet.

"Lana!" Bub shouted.

My heart leapt into my throat, and tears poured from my eyes. "Up here." I choked the words out and had to try twice more before I was sure he had heard me.

A buzzing swarm spilled through the door, slamming it back against the wall, and then Bub materialized. He gasped and knelt before me, his hands touching my face first and then my shoulders, searching my body for injuries. When he worked his way back up to my head, and his fingers prodded the tender spot on my skull, I winced.

"I'm okay," I said. "Just a concussion. My shoulders hurt worse."

Bub's concerned face hardened a bit. He pulled a knife from his boot and sliced through the rope around my wrists. My shoulders ached as they fell forward and the circulation returned to my arms, renewing my grateful tears.

"I thought you were dead," Bub hissed through clenched teeth. "You have—*had*—a soulish doppelganger. And she was wearing the jacket I helped you pick out." He sucked in a tense breath and then wrapped his arms around my shoulders, crushing me to his chest. "Don't ever go off to save the world without me again. *Ever.* Do you hear?"

"After the night I've had, the world can burn," I said, only half joking. "How did you find me?"

"That rebel harlot you helped escape last spring."

"Tasha?" I pulled away to look at him. "She tracked you down?"

Bub raised an eyebrow. "Naledi helped me track *her* down. I'm amazed she hasn't been caught by the guard. She's rather careless about revisiting places that are compromised, isn't she?"

I shrugged, grimacing when my shoulders protested. "How many casualties are downstairs?" I asked next, not sure I wanted to know the answer.

Bub's face turned somber. "It was a massacre, love. Counting them will take time we don't have."

"Time we don't have?" I echoed back. He stood and helped me to my feet.

"The throne realm is broken—"

"I know."

"—and Naledi is missing."

"What? But she called you. You said she helped you find Tasha." I shook my head, unable to believe this was happening.

"She did," Bub said. "She also called Gabriel and Kevin. And Maalik," he added, the fear in his expression outweighing jealousy. "They're searching the city for her now. We need to return and help."

"Vince and Ruth," I said, turning toward the open door. "They just agreed to free me and bring their souls to Naledi in the throne realm."

Bub touched my arm. "They're gone, love. There's nothing more we can do here."

"They had six original believers. We need to know if any of them survived."

"You won't be able to pick them out. Your soul vision…" He let the sentence hang, knowing I could fill in the rest. The council had screwed the pooch big time.

"Dirty bastards," I grumbled under my breath.

Bub nodded knowingly. "Let's go, love."

"Not yet." I stalked across the room and grabbed my knife off the desk, tucking it back in my boot where it belonged. Then I headed for the door. Bub followed close behind.

Outside the office was a small, metal balcony attached to a set of stairs that led down into the warehouse proper. Yellow paint chipped off the railing, revealing several layers of various colors beneath. The upkeep of it had been so neglected, I didn't realize that the abundance of red as it neared the ground level was blood until my eyes took in the bodies layered across the warehouse floor.

I'd been a reaper for over three hundred years, and I had put in plenty of long hours on the Posy Unit, so I was no stranger to carnage. But the sight took my breath away. There had to be a thousand souls in the warehouse. Many of them were withered and blackened, like they'd been caught in a giant furnace and burned for so long that their skeletons had shriveled down to doll-sized proportions. Only a few were left in recognizable condition, and as I did the math, I understood why.

Six souls had been dismembered, their heads torn away from their bodies, the noggins nowhere to be found. I couldn't see their unique auras, and I had a feeling I wouldn't have been able to even if Naledi hadn't revoked my special vision. Grim had sucked them dry. I could feel it in my bones. Somehow, this was so much worse than a human death. There was no coming back from this. Not for anyone. Not ever.

Vince and Ruth had survived the scorching and decapitation, but they were just as dead as everyone else. Vince was sprawled backwards over a piece of machinery, his head twisted around at an unnatural angle, and one knee bent the wrong way. His vacant, gray eyes looked surprised. Like he couldn't believe how fast it had all happened. I knew I couldn't.

Ruth lay face-up over a pile of bodies not far away. My jacket had slipped down her arms, and one sleeve was torn across the elbow. A ragged hole in her chest made me visualize Grim tearing her heart out with his bare hands, and I shuddered. I was ready to be out of there, but I needed the skeleton coin. I raced over to Ruth's body and dug my hand down into the jacket pocket—first one, and then the other.

"Leave it, love," Bub shouted from the stairs. A disgusted look stained his face as he took in the room a second time. "You have other jackets."

"I'm not after the jacket." My fingers closed around the coin, and I held it up for him to see.

As I crossed the room, I couldn't help but pause to give Vince one last look. We'd almost fixed this mess. Or we'd almost had the chance to. Now, we'd never know. Either way, he wasn't the enemy. Not anymore. I put a gentle hand to his cheek.

"I'll make this right," I said, not just to Vince, but to them all. It wasn't only Saul who needed to be avenged now. And while I was plenty terrified of Grim, I wasn't tied up any longer. And I had a knife.

And one hell of a handsome demon who had my back, I added mentally, stepping up beside Bub. He wrapped an arm around my waist, and I flipped the skeleton coin, taking us directly to the throne realm.

Even though I'd already seen the molested sky here, it took me by surprise. The angry rift that separated night and day seemed to have widened, but the rain had stopped. The ground was wet and muddy, and it reminded me of the soggy graveyard in Atlanta.

"The others are in the city," Bub said, giving me a questioning look.

"Naledi was supposed to be here. She was going to fix that." I pointed up at the celestial damage. "I don't know where else she would have gone, so best to start here. Let's check the cottage."

We headed across the lawn and up the front porch. The front door hung open, and I wondered if Naledi had come back through here or if this was how we'd left it. The foyer looked untouched. The living room, too. In the kitchen, I found a serving tray stacked with unwashed teacups and saucers, likely leftover from the Apparition Agency meeting she'd hosted before I arrived and all hell broke loose.

"I'm sure the others checked this realm thoroughly," Bub said. "We should be searching new terrain, covering more ground."

I sighed and headed back outside. I was missing something. It had to be here. I felt it pulling at me. My eyes were drawn back up to the sky again and the gaping void that divided two halves of a whole. Except, it wasn't a void at all.

Beyond the shadows of the furled edges of the atmosphere, I could see golden leaves rustling in a gentle wind. A twinkle of light slipped through them, and my breath caught. It was the light set into the hand of Coreen's memorial statue.

"There," I whispered, pointing it out to Bub. "We need to go there."

He hesitated. "We don't know what's through there."

"I do," I insisted. "And we need to go now. It's happening now."

I could feel the pull again, like an invisible hand clenching around my insides and dragging me toward my destiny. There was something I had to do. I wasn't sure what it was yet, but I would know it when I saw it. At least, I hoped I would.

Bub pressed his lips to mine in a sudden kiss, and then his dark eyes locked on mine, the flecks of gold swirling anxiously. "Take your coin. I'll go in first and buy you some extra time." He dissolved into his swarm slowly, the flies pixelating him from the feet up, leaving his longing eyes for last.

I wanted to go with him, hand in hand like a terrified child, but he was right. Taking on Grim was going to require every advantage we could summon. And maybe a few more that we couldn't. I had a horrible feeling that I knew where Naledi was, and that she was responsible for the invisible leash on my psyche.

I took a deep breath and flipped the skeleton coin.

CHAPTER TWENTY-FOUR

"A man who won't die for something is not fit to live."
—Martin Luther King, Jr.

Limbo City was in rare form. The trees in the park thrashed in a wind unlike any they'd ever encountered before. Branches creaked and snapped, littering the ground around Saul's and Coreen's memorial statues, and leaves were violently shaken from their limbs before being dragged into a blinding windstorm. The park lights flickered as if the electricity might go out any minute.

I had the skeleton coin drop me off in the space behind Josie's marble bench. It seemed like it would be good cover, but with the flurry of leaves and the erratic lighting, I couldn't see anything. The wind was cruel, and without a jacket, it assaulted me with its icy gusts, instantly chapping my lips and drawing water from my eyes.

"Lana!"

I thought Bub was shouting my name, but the wind distorted my hearing as well as my sight. When a hand latched on to my shoulder, I almost pissed myself. Naledi knelt beside me, taking shelter from the onslaught of leaves. Her coil of braids had come loose, and they spilled over her shoulders, writhing against the wind like Medusa's serpents.

"Lana, you made it," she said, relief trembling her voice. "Where are the souls? We need them."

My heart lurched, and Naledi found the answer in my expression. "I'm sorry," I said. "What do we do now?"

Naledi's gaze fell away from mine, her mournful eyes searching the storm raging through the park. "There's nothing we *can* do," she said, so softly that I almost didn't hear her over the roar of the wind.

My eyes rolled up to the tear in the sky, visible through the spinning leaves and the treetops as their limbs grew barren. It was less visible over the city, camouflaged by the cover of night. It looked like a wispy cloud. Or like the blur of the Milky Way that I sometimes spied from the viewing ledge up the mountain trail behind the manor in Tartarus.

"I thought you were going to fix that," I said to Naledi, frowning as I looked back to her.

She was crying, silent tears trailing down her cheeks, the wind hastening their journey across her dark skin. "I thought I could," she said. Her voice rose over the howling wind. "But it's not just the realm that's broken."

My pulse quickened as I huddled in closer to her, trying to understand what she was saying. I just wanted something to make sense, but it was hard to focus in the mayhem. My hand gripped the back of Josie's marble bench. It felt like ice, but it was the only thing grounding me. The wind ripped at my curls and played tug of war with the air in my chest, sucking the breath from my mouth any time I tried to speak.

Naledi gripped my forearm, drawing my focus back to her soulful eyes. "As above, so below," she whispered, pushing the words into my mind by will rather than volume.

The park lights stuttered, and the leaves seemed to freeze in the air around us, flickering in slow motion as if someone had plunged a disco ball underwater. But the sudden silence was most jarring.

"As above, so below," Naledi said again, her voice sharp and clear. "Too many originals have been lost. I am the last pillar of the middle ground. The balance of Eternity's power falls to the souls of the sea. The throne reflects above what they hold below."

I shook my head, trying to let her know that I was an idiot. That I didn't have the slightest idea what she was talking about. That none of what she said gave me half a fucking clue what I should be doing to stop the madness closing in around us.

Naledi's hold on my arm tightened, her fingernails biting into my skin. "*Listen*," she snapped, cutting me off before I could spill my confessions. "When Grim takes the throne, don't think, just do. *This* is what you were made for."

"*When* he takes the throne?" My breath rushed out like I'd been slugged in the stomach and I curled in on myself, shying away from the storm as it filled in around us, reclaiming the silence and ending our reprieve.

"Naledi." A booming voice cut through the storm. It doubled me over a second time, and I shrank behind Josie's bench, trying to learn how to disappear.

A deep, whooshing sound like a helicopter's blades cut through the air, and then Grim's black wings opened over the memorial garden. His milky complexion glowed against the darkness, purple veins throbbing beneath translucent skin. His nakedness seemed to suggest that he'd regressed back to his most primal origins, and his eyes were full black as if they hadn't returned to their normal state since the first bloodbath in the throne realm.

Panic shot through me as he landed in the clearing before the bronze statues. The leaves didn't touch him, and I realized the spot was a vacuum, the center from which the storm pushed outward.

Grim's black eyes searched the park, pausing as they reached the bench Naledi and I cowered behind. I couldn't flip a coin in this wind. There was no escape, and the look on Naledi's face told me she wasn't interested in one. Her hand softened on my arm, and she ran it up to my shoulder and then to my cheek.

"Remember to listen." She gave me a tender smile and stood. The storm parted for her, leaves curling away to form a clear path toward Grim and the statues.

"What are you doing?" I stumbled from the shelter of the bench to reach after her. But the path closed at her back, a blur of golden leaves and bitter-cold air rushing in to fill the emptiness.

"Naledi!" I held my arm over my face and cried out to her, squinting through the coarse debris. It felt like shrapnel exploding around me on a battlefield. As if nature had chosen a side, and it wasn't mine.

The noise intensified in my ears, and voices crept in to join the chaos. A howl broke the din, and then Saul's gritty tongue licked my elbow. My hound wedged his big, black head under my arm and took refuge from the storm. I held him close, soaking in the warmth of his fur. My skin had taken on a bluish tint from the cold, and I suddenly wondered what the odds were of me dying from hypothermia tonight. Right now, it sounded better than the alternative deaths plaguing my mind.

Another howl ripped through the air, and I looked up to see Coreen barrel past us, ignoring the onslaught of the storm as she raced across the destroyed garden. As she darted around Naledi, her lips peeled back from her muzzle in a vicious snarl, and my heart swelled with pride at her determination and bravery. She paused at the feet of the bronze statues, her back bunching up like a loaded spring, and then she launched herself at Grim.

It was clear he hadn't expected the attack. Coreen's jaws closed over his shoulder, biting down where it met his neck and piercing through his collarbone. But the sound he made was more rage than pain. His wings shot out from his back and thrust downward, lifting them both into the sky.

Coreen kicked her back feet up at his torso as she tried to hang on, but Grim's thrashing finally shook her loose. She fell to the ground, landing on her back with a wounded yip. She rolled over and tried to pull herself up again, but Grim's foot connected with her spine.

A sickening crackle of bones made my heart spasm, and then Saul tore away from my arms. He followed his sister's path through the storm, curling around Naledi as she continued her slow progression, and rushed up behind where Grim loomed over Coreen.

But Grim would not be taken by surprise a second time. He turned his wrath on my hound, taking to the air again as he kicked Saul under the ribcage. Before Saul could gain his footing, Grim wrapped his hand around the hound's collar and hurled him across the park and into the base of a tulip tree. The trunk splintered, causing the tree to sway more violently, and for a moment, I wondered if the whole thing might break free and be sucked into the vortex spiraling around the park.

The storm was escalating, the gale-force winds building into some terrible climax. The lighter wooden benches that encircled the memorial garden scraped along the concrete, and the fur ruffled across the motionless bodies of my hounds. I wanted to run to them, to take them up in my arms before they were swept away. I had the desire to bury my face in their fur and sob myself into hysterics until this whole nightmare was over.

But more than that, I wanted to sink my knife into Grim's face and tear off his wings. Wrath boiled up in my chest, filling my mouth with a bitter taste. I stood up slowly from behind Josie's bench and glared at him through the fragmented chaos. The raging winds had crushed the leaves, crumbling the drier ones into a gritty powder that made me feel like I was sinking in quicksand.

Grim hovered in the clean air above the memorial garden, untouched by the land's fury. Dark blood oozed from the puncture wounds Coreen had inflicted. It trailed down his chest and one arm, marring his otherwise perfect flesh. His black eyes seemed to take in everything, but the tilt of his chin revealed the brunt of his focus.

Naledi continued to advance toward the bronze statues. Her burlap dress billowed at her feet, and her braids whipped around her face and shoulders. Her progression was slow and methodical, like a bride approaching her groom. What the *hell* was wrong with her?

"Has she lost her mind?" Gabriel yelled as he landed behind me. His wings drew up on either side as I turned around, shielding me from the worst of the storm, and I wrapped my arms around his neck in a fierce hug. His blond curls were mangled from the wind, but his skin felt hot under mine, and he shivered against my icy embrace.

"We have to stop him," I shouted in Gabriel's ear, trying to be heard over the storm.

He nodded gravely and withdrew the sword at his hip. "Stay here," he said, and then lifted into the air.

I gasped as the debris pelted me again. It felt harsher than before. I dropped back down behind Josie's bench and covered my ears, watching as Gabriel charged Grim. This was madness, and certainly no time for a fair fight. We needed to assault Grim all at once, I thought, just as Bub's army of flies swarmed the god's face.

Grim shook his head, looking mildly annoyed, but still managed to dodge Gabriel's sword and delivered a solid blow to the angel's temple. Grim reared his fist back as if to strike again, when an arrowhead blossomed through his chest, just under his left nipple. His back bowed, and he twisted in the air, looking for the source of his pain.

Gabriel came in for another jab with his sword, but Grim caught the end of it in one hand, wrenching it away from the angel. He spun in a wide arc, searching the ground for perpetrators. When his eyes found me, they widened. Those glossy black orbs took me in with some strange mixture of rage and delight. Something else swirled around in there, perhaps fear or derangement, but it seemed unimportant as Grim hurled the sword in my direction. I sucked in a startled breath and tried to dodge its trajectory.

Silver wings hissed through the air, and then Maalik collapsed on the ground with a gurgling moan. The hilt of Gabriel's sword was buried in his stomach. He lay on his side, convulsing as his wings flapped frantically in the thrashing winds.

I reached down to him, clenching and unclenching my fingers, not knowing what else to do. My breath panted in and out in ragged succession, and horror consumed me as blood trickled from Maalik's mouth and the fire in his eyes burned out.

Tears blurred my vision. I looked up, seeking out Grim. The dire situation in the sky had grown while I'd been busy watching Maalik take his final breaths. But Grim was still on top. I realized that right away. Grim grasped Bub's throat in one hand, and Gabriel's in his other, their bodies dangling limply. It was as if he had been waiting for me to look up and see what he had done. He released them, letting them fall to the ground below, and my heart exploded with despair.

There were more bodies scattered throughout the garden. I could see them now that my eyes searched the carnage for Bub and Gabriel. Grim worked fast. And now I was suddenly alone, with nothing standing between me and his ire.

Except Naledi.

I watched as she stopped before the memorial statues and turned her gaze up to Grim. She held her hand out to him in polite invitation.

This couldn't be happening. Denial was the only thing holding my sanity together. Everything else was too overwhelming. Grief and heartache and terror, turning my stomach into a ball of furious energy. A sudden pressure in my chest filled me with blistering heat. It rolled down my arms and sent a pins and needles sensation throughout my body as it chased away the chill in my core.

Listen. Naledi turned and gave me a meaningful look. The storm hushed as Grim descended on her, and the leaves and debris slowed their furious spiral. The fire in my chest was almost too much without the freezing wind to mollify it.

Grim's feet touched down lightly in the clearing before the statues. His back was to me, and I caught a glimpse of the arrow protruding from his ribcage before his great black wings folded over his shoulders like a cloak. He took Naledi in his arms like a lover, and she let him.

I wanted to scream at her. How could she do this? Everyone had fought so hard. How could she just give up?

Grim reached one hand up and stroked it down the side of her face and across her neck. I held my breath, waiting for the ugly part to come. The part where he would twist her head off and suck her essence out through her eye sockets. The part where the world would collapse in on itself.

Instead, he leaned in close as if to kiss Naledi. When she opened her mouth to him, his eyes closed. Blue light spilled from her. It washed over Grim, encasing him in a cocoon of tranquil power. It was beautiful and horrifying all at once.

I was startled out of my daze when I caught Naledi staring at me over Grim's shoulder. Her eyes were full of that blue light, transferring it slowly into him, and the message she'd been trying to send me was clear. She was sacrificing herself to create a window. This would be the only chance I had to stop this nightmare.

I took a timid step away from Josie's marble bench. The soft earth and mulched leaves crunched beneath my boots, and I knew I'd never be able to sneak up behind Grim. But with the storm gone, my options expanded.

I pulled the skeleton coin from my pocket and flipped it in the air.

When I appeared behind Grim, Naledi was gone, reduced to nothing more than soul matter coursing through a power-drunk god. The ground beneath us trembled with conse-quence, and I feared I was too late. I *knew* I was too late.

The dead littering the park filled my heart with immeas-urable grief that amplified as my focus returned to Grim. The adrenaline shooting through my veins ignited the spark in my chest. Heat radiated through me, and I felt like I'd been dosed with boiling water.

My hands glowed red like they had the few other times I'd used them to pull someone out of existence. I lifted them, turning my palms over with detached wonder. The fiery light spilled over Grim's shoulder, and he turned toward me, surprise breaking the sated look on his face.

As I plunged my hands through the blue light and his bare chest, the most brilliant colors spilled out of him. And into me.

I pulled away, expecting the ethereal pop of energy and dispersal of soul matter that should have followed, but I was stuck. My hands wouldn't budge. Grim stared at me with wide eyes. I pulled harder, straining to twist away from him, expecting a retaliating blow that never came.

The colorful light kept unraveling from him, like knotted scarves from a clown's breast pocket. It felt like it could go on forever, and I had a moment of panic thinking that it might until Grim's luminosity began to fade. His skin turned sallow and ashen, and then as the last of the light trickled from him, his body crumbled in on itself, fading into dust.

Relief washed over me, but it didn't last. The light was still settling inside my core, and with it, a thousand voices broke the surface of my mind.

CHAPTER TWENTY·FIVE

"Between us and heaven or hell there is only life,
which is the frailest thing in the world."
—*Blaise Pascal*

The noise in my head was unbearable. Voices in dozens of languages I couldn't understand flooded my mind. They wouldn't shut up. How could anyone function like this?

I caught snippets of English, French, and Latin, three languages that I knew, but they were quickly drowned out by the scrambled din of nonsense. Pressure pushed at the back of my eyes, and pain radiated along the circumference of my skull, pulsing more quickly as the voices grew louder. Urgent and angry. They wanted to know why I wasn't listening. I could understand that much.

Maybe if I bashed my head against something... My sanity wasn't that far gone. Yet. But it was getting close enough that I began to panic. My own memories nagged at the edge of my consciousness, but I couldn't reach them. Not through the voices that demanded precedence.

I looked down at my open palms. They were glowing. Light spilled from my fingers, turning night to day, and it illuminated the dead bodies lying around the garden, spread in a circle all around me.

I recognized these beings, on some basic level. Angels, a demon, hellhounds, reapers. *Reapers.* That's what I was. I was a reaper. This power didn't belong to me. It was meant for something else. But the longer I held onto it, the harder it was to understand what I had to do with it.

Something instinctual passed through me, and I pointed a finger at the slain demon lying across the carpet of bright leaves. Energy flowed out of me in a subtle mist, covering him in white light. He inhaled a sharp breath, and then his eyes opened, taking me in with fearful wonder.

"Lana," he whispered.

It was my name. The voices echoed it back and forth inside my head, inflected with various accents, but otherwise, the same word. A moment of clarity took hold of my mind, and I shook with anticipation as I threw my hands out, hoping to repeat the deed that had delivered a morsel of salvation.

White light shot forth from me in a rolling wave, and all at once, the other beings woke with life. At the same time, I felt life wane inside me. If I could only give away more, then this pain might end. I might remember who I was. Because I was certainly someone. I could tell from the recognition set in the surprised faces that encircled me.

Memories filtered through in the moments of solace I'd purchased with the light. I knew more than my name. I knew this city. I knew these people. And I knew what had to be done. I stepped over the pile of ash at my feet and walked toward the Sea of Eternity.

"Lana?" Confused voices called behind me, but I couldn't be dissuaded or postponed. The noise in my head would come back soon, and I would forget all over again. This had to be done now.

The strange light lit my way, and the others followed me to the edge of the water where it touched a rocky stretch of soil. I stepped into the sea and felt hands skim over my feet. More reached for me as I ventured out farther.

"What is she doing?" someone asked behind me. Did I even know? Something instructed me from within. I hadn't heard her at first, layered in with the other voices, but she'd finally found her way to the forefront.

Listen.

Naledi invaded my thoughts.

Give the light to the sea, she whispered.

And so, I did. I thrust my hands into the water and let go. The light wasn't mine anyway, and I didn't want it. It hurt, but it didn't mean to. It didn't have to. Some forces of nature just weren't meant to be tamed.

The light shot out beneath the water, glistening and sparkling as it spread away from me. The seafloor trembled with the weight of it, and the intense power reached out to the sky, calling forth an early dawn. In the distance, a series of small islands broke the surface of the sea, dotting the horizon. They were green and lush. As I watched, a soul crawled up out of the water and onto one of the sandy beaches. And then another. Together, they reached down and helped a third join them.

I smiled at the sight, thinking of my friends. I remembered them now, as the last of the light left me, and I turned around to face them.

"What have you done?" Ridwan said, his wings fluttering uneasily. So, maybe they weren't all friends.

"What should have been done a long time ago," I said, walking back up the rocky shore. My legs felt heavy, the way they did after a long run through the desert with Bub and the hounds.

Speaking of my devil, he ran past the others and pulled me into his arms. I could feel his frantic heart beating against my chest, and my own swelled as I recalled how close I had been to losing him. He didn't say anything as he held me close, and I realized this was the first time I had rendered him completely speechless.

The hounds were only a few steps behind, and even Coreen rushed to greet me, her muzzle seeking out my hand with an eager whimper. Gabriel nudged her out of the way as he threw his own arms around me, dragging Bub into a group hug with us, and Kevin soon followed suit. Maalik and Jenni seemed content to watch from farther up the beach, their wary eyes focused on the new islands in the distance. Ridwan stood with them, watching our public display of affection with equal parts horror, disgust, and confusion.

"Where's Naledi?" Jenni asked after we'd disentangled ourselves and headed up to the end of Market Street where it met Factory Bend.

My heart pinched. "She's gone. Grim got to her before I could stop him," I said softly, shame filling me despite how many I'd just resurrected.

"Then who's on the throne?" Ridwan demanded to know.

"No one."

"What?" he spluttered. "Well someone has to be on the throne. You'll have to find an original believer to replace Naledi, immediately."

I barked out a laugh, and his wings twitched as if startled.

"The council took away my ability to see a soul's aura," I reminded him. "I couldn't track down an original believer even if I wanted to. And even if one did happen to fall in our laps, it wouldn't do any good. The throne is broken."

"What?" Jenni cocked her head at me. "What do you mean it's broken?"

I turned and glanced across the sea to the new islands. "I mean there's nothing for anyone to sit on. The power of the throne now resides in the sea. It *is* the sea."

"How are we supposed to distribute the soul matter?" Ridwan was all up in arms.

"You're not," I said. "It will flow into the sea."

"That's preposterous!" He stomped his foot, and his wings unfurled and flapped against his back in irritation. I saw Maalik grin from the corner of my eye.

"You stole my gift and then shut down my unit. What did you think would come of that? There's nothing more I can do for you, and it's your own fault."

Ridwan took a step toward me, but then he hesitated as if remembering what I'd done in the park. If he thought I still possessed that power, I'd let him believe it. His reluctance might have also had something to do with Gabriel and Bub flanking me.

Voices echoed across the water behind us, and we all turned to see what new developments were occurring on the first island. A dozen souls now stood on the beach, laughing and hugging each other. The energy I'd given to the sea was pure, and I knew the souls affected were worthy. If the godless could build their own paradise, maybe there was hope for us all.

"Is that Nessa?" Kevin nudged me and nodded down the street.

The tiny brownie was swearing at the padlock on the sliding door of her donut shop. My watch showed that it was just past four a.m., but the sky over Limbo City looked like it could be nearing noon. I wondered if this would alter the city's night and day schedule. And then I decided I didn't care. That was the council's problem.

"Someone's buying me breakfast," I said. I linked my hand in Bub's and dragged him toward the donut shop. Gabriel and Kevin trailed behind us, with the hounds running laps back and forth in between. We looked like hell—clothing ripped, hair askew, blood and dirt smeared everywhere.

Maalik, Ridwan, and Jenni stayed behind—plenty of strange, new political things to sort out, I was sure. *Not my problem.* I kept reminding myself that.

Nessa glanced up as our strange party neared her shop. She was so flustered from her struggle with the lock that she didn't even notice our battle-worn condition. She rolled up the metal door over the front window and hurried inside. "Be with ye in just a moment. Most sincere apologies. I must have overslept this morning."

Gabriel scratched his cheek and threw an arm over my shoulder. "Hey, Nes, are you hiring?" She gave him a strange look, though it couldn't have been any stranger than mine. Gabriel snorted. "I don't think there has ever been a better time to get out of politics. And the council, well, without the extra soul matter to bicker over, they might as well be wearing prom crowns."

Bub blubbered out a startled laugh, the first sound he'd made since saying my name after he'd been resurrected. "A prom crown. That's brilliant. I should have one sent to Cindy."

A dazed expression still clung to his face, but I was sure a little sugary goodness would perk us all up. And then I was going to let Jenni know I'd be taking the rest of the day off. I needed a nap. If she tried to stop me, I'd threaten to leave her be the next time a demented god killed her dead. Not that I'd be resurrecting anyone. Ever again.

The concentrated soul matter that had passed from one throne soul to the next was gone, distributed beneath the sea, and destined to become whatever the souls molded it into. As I watched them gather on the islands to celebrate their new existence, I daydreamed about all the possibilities. The borders of Eternity weren't going anywhere, and neither were the deities, but Vince had been right to some degree. The souls needed reformation, and they deserved it.

And that's what I'd been made for. I knew it now more than ever.

CHAPTER TWENTY-SIX

*"I think I will be able to, in the end, rise above
the clouds and climb the stairs to Heaven,
and I will look down on my beautiful life."*
—Yayoi Kusama

The very last generation of reapers lined up in front of the stage at the one thousand, three hundred and second Oracle Ball. It was a bittersweet moment, and one that I was glad to be present for, even with the slew of cautious glances coming at me from every angle of the Reapers Inc. rooftop.

"Smile, love," Bub whispered through his teeth.

We were seated at a table near the back, mostly because I wanted to bolt as soon as the ceremony was over. I'd promised Jenni that I would make an appearance, and while I was so over the council's pomp and circumstance, I did look forward to getting a peek at the new reaper generation.

Kevin sat at the table with us. He was stag tonight, his platonic plans to go with Ellen having been thwarted by Ross. The captain of the Nephilim Guard wore his armor to the ball, though he'd left his helmet at the coat check. Ellen had found a slinky, gold, mermaid dress to match—a last-minute deal at Athena's.

Gabriel and Amy were at the table with us, too. Gabriel in his standard, white robe, and Amy in a flaming-red tango number. They were night and day, that pair. But they made it look good.

"Good evening," Jenni said into the microphone at the stage podium.

The council sat in a row behind her, but none of them looked especially thrilled to be there. A rumor was going around that several of them were petitioning for shorter terms, not wanting to waste their precious time now that the positions had been rendered so useless. Meng Po was the only one I cared to see stick around. Parvati and Athena weren't so bad either, I guess. Maalik...

The angel had hit every high and low on the spectrum of my tolerance. He'd killed my mentor. And then he'd saved my life. He'd done a dozen other perplexing things in between. Forgiveness felt like too strong of a word. But maybe we were at least even. As long as he stayed out of my way, I'd stay out of his.

His brother, on the other hand, could take a long walk off a short pier at the lake of fire in Hell. He could take Holly Spirit with him. And Cindy Morningstar could go dunk her head in a vat of holy water.

The new reapers in front of the stage glanced across the rooftop, taking in the strange variety of guests as Jenni announced them. There were nine in all, and a nervous energy surrounded them. As the very last generation of reapers, it looked like we were going to need a reformation of our own soon. I had a feeling that Warren's soul gauntlet would come into play—though I wouldn't be taking the next prototype out for a test run. He still wasn't speaking to me.

"Eliza Lockwood," Jenni announced, pausing as her eyes met mine. I blinked at her in confusion. "With the highest score on the L&L exam and superior marks in soul relations, you'll be serving your apprenticeship alongside Kevin Kraus under Lana Harvey."

The room flooded with applause, but I was too stunned to join in. Ellen was still under my guidance, and now I had a second apprentice? What was Jenni trying to do to me?

I forced the tension out of my shoulders and tried to smile as the new girl approached our table. Her short tufts of hair made me think of Josie, but her dark skin and honey-colored eyes were all Naledi. My throat tightened.

"Pleased to meet you," Eliza said. Her robe was too long in the sleeves, so she tugged one up to reach out and shake my hand.

"Likewise," I said, actually meaning it.

Maybe this wouldn't be so bad. After all, Kevin had come a long way in a short time. That meant I was good at this mentoring gig, right? Maybe I was still riding the residual high of being alive after almost certain death, but I was going to take this move of Jenni's as compliment instead of punishment.

The rest of the reapers in front of the stage found their mentors, and then I zoned out for a while as Jenni rattled off a vague explanation for the new islands and announced the council's changed status. She'd already practiced it on me too many times to count.

The details were still coming together, but it had at least been decided that a soul from the Isles of Eternity, as they were being called, would join the council at some point in the near future. A factory soul would be coming on board too, along with a nephilim, and a reaper, bringing the total number on the new council to thirteen, with Jenni serving as mediator. It seemed like a good start to me.

As soon as Jenni finished with the boring formalities of the evening, I let Bub drag me out on the dance floor. The band fired up, playing some funky jazz number, and we bounced around under the glow of lanterns until we broke a sweat and the crystal bands in my hair slid around, loosening my pinned curls.

Bub pulled me in close when a slow song began, begging for one more dance. The lights dimmed, and the silver sequins on his vest and the bodice of my dress sparkled in the dark, making us glow like a nightlight on the rooftop. I pressed my cheek to his and closed my eyes, enjoying the moment and forgetting the rest of the world spinning around us.

A short while later, we danced again, only this time it was on the deck of the ship. Kevin had arranged an after party for our nearest and dearest. He'd coiled string lights around the railings and up the masts, and several ice-packed coolers had been loaded with Ambrosia Ale. A radio on the forecastle had been tuned to the Fallen Frequency station in Hell, and rock ballads crooned out over the ship and harbor, mixing with excited voices and laughter, and the occasional bark of a hellhound or helljack.

I stood at the back of the poop deck, gazing across the sea at the flickering lights on the beaches in the distance. I wondered how the new souls were doing. I hadn't had much of a chance to visit with them yet, as Jenni and the council wanted to establish some ground rules first. *Blah-ditty, blah.* I rolled my eyes thinking of their ridiculousness.

"Kevin's about to make a toast, love." Bub slipped up beside me and held out a bottle of Ambrosia Ale. I took it from him, slipping my free hand in his, and followed him down to the main deck where everyone waited.

My newest apprentice had discarded her ill-fitting robe, revealing a green, off-the-shoulder sweater dress. A pair of phoenix feather earrings hung from her lobes, and I was willing to bet my skeleton coin they'd come from Ellen, who sat next to Eliza on the edge of the forecastle deck. Ross dug through a cooler and loaded his arms with a few bottles before flying back up to join them just as Gabriel spotted me and turned down the radio. He nudged Kevin.

"There she is," Kevin said, raising his bottle of ale in greeting. "Our fearless leader."

I chuckled at his words, but no one else seemed to take him as ironically as I did. Eyes full of respect and awe and gratitude turned to take me in, and I realized there were far more guests present than Kevin had led me to believe were coming. Way more.

Apollo and Anubis caught my attention as they climbed up the ramp and filtered into the crowd on the deck. And Meng Po, Jack, and Jai Ling sat together atop the hatch platform. I spotted Jenni, Asmodeus, Adrianna—there were at least fifty more people I hadn't expected to see.

"I think that's everyone now," Kevin said, breaking my startled trance. "We're all gathered here tonight not just to celebrate the new generation of reapers or another trip around the sun with the mortals, but to honor the one who made this night and every night after possible. Lana Harvey, my mentor and dear friend, who has saved my life—and many lives on this ship tonight—"

"Here, here!" shouted Asmodeus. Apollo lifted his bottle of ale at me in silent gratitude, and Jai Ling patted her hand to her heart. Even Jenni nodded at me.

"—so tonight," Kevin continued, "we also celebrate Lana, for her bravery and friendship, for slaying the grimmest of reapers, and for bringing a little more peace and justice to this strange world of ours. She's done more for Eternity than most will ever know."

Everyone cheered and lifted their beverages in my direction. I lifted mine in return and gave them an awkward smile as I took a drink.

The praise felt strange. As if maybe it wasn't enough. Or maybe it was too much. I couldn't decide.

Oh, that which I had endured. That which I had conquered. Yet, if things had turned out differently, even in the slightest, it could have been Saul or Vince standing here in my place. Josie or Coreen. Possibly even Grim, in some skewed version.

I was nothing special. But I guess that's how these things worked. Maybe heroes were sometimes clumsy and unwilling, and maybe villains could be well-intentioned. It's all in the angle from which one looks. All in how we choose to remember the events that shape our world.

A thousand years from now, I might be remembered as a grand hero with my own likeness molded in bronze in the center of some park. Or my name could be whispered in the shadows, an infamous figure that marked the beginning of a great depression or the collapse of Eternity's infrastructure. Then again, I might not be remembered at all.

Bub winked at me from across the deck of the ship, and I decided maybe that wouldn't be so bad. Eternity could find a new hero. It was in no short supply of fresh faces. Maybe a soul would take up the helm next.

Or maybe even you.

Missing Lana and the gang already? Check out all their side jobs in…

LIMBO CITY LIGHTS

A Lana Harvey, Reapers Inc. Short Story Collection

Available Now in Print, eBook, and Audio!

The complete collection of Lana Harvey, Reapers Inc. short stories! Including the 3 previously published shorts: *Dearly Departed*, *Hair of the Hellhound*, and *Season's Reapings*, PLUS 3 all-new shorts: *Pre-Mortem* (set in the 1700s), *Post-Mortem* (set in the 2300s), and *Death or Something Like It*, a crossover short story with Jesse Sullivan, the heroine of Kory M. Shrum's *Dying for a Living* series.

ACKNOWLEDGMENTS

2019 10-year anniversary update: I can hardly believe that Lana turns 10 this year! To celebrate, I asked Rebecca Frank to revamp the cover designs, my cousin Kaitlyn Beck to pose as Lana, my husband Paul to photograph her, and my editor Chelle Olson to clean up my early work that I heavily relied on English-savvy teacher pals to proofread back in the day. I also can't forget shout-outs to Hollie Jackson, the epic narrator who voices Lana in the audiobooks; the Four Horsemen of the Bookocalypse, my amazing critique group; and THE professor George Shelley, whose enthusiasm for Lana's world motivated me at times I'd almost given up on writing. All my gratitude to you wonderful mavens who make my books shine and my heart swell.

Original acknowledgments: It's kind of weird and bittersweet saying goodbye to Lana and Limbo City. Lana would have never made it this far if not for the wonderful readers who have supported me through the years, sending encouraging emails to express their enthusiasm for the series and leaving reviews online. You guys are truly the best, and I hope that you'll follow me into the brave new worlds I'll be exploring next.

Many, many thanks to Professor George Shelley, for keeping Lana grammatically in check and for the wonderful, bookish conversations over coffee. I'm so glad that we've stayed in touch, and I sincerely miss your comp class. Learning is easy when you have clever instructors who are passionate about what they teach.

Another mountain of gratitude goes to the Four Horsemen of the Bookocalypse: Kory M. Shrum, Monica La Porta, and Katie Pendleton. Thank you so much for catching my typos (even when I'm super late with my manuscripts) and for your friendship and your expertise in this crazy new publishing world. It seems less chaotic with our four heads put together.

Extra appreciation shout-outs to: Andrea Cook for the epic Twitter countdowns, Jill Wade for the industry insight coffee dates at the bookstore, Bruce Brodnax for the great typo catches and fun email conversations, Robin Phillips for your friendship and for always coming to my Sedalia signings, my mom and dad for watching my little minion during those signings…

And last, but never least, thanks goes to my husband, Paul, for suffering through the weird story ideas I ramble on about, for the proofreading, for taking care of the house and our kiddo while I have conversations with my imaginary friends in my office, for driving long hours with me to conventions and signings, for dressing up like the Grim Reaper and passing out bookmarks, for giving my card out to damn near every stranger (stranger? what's that?) and telling them to read my books, for being my biggest cheerleader, for being my best friend, for being my everything. I couldn't have pulled any of this off without you by my side. These books should probably have your name on the cover along with mine for as much work as you've put into making all of this happen. I love you so very much.

ABOUT THE AUTHOR

USA Today bestselling author **Angela Roquet** is a great big weirdo. She collects Danger Girl comic books, owls, skulls, random craft supplies, and all things Joss Whedon. She's a fan of renewable energy, marriage equality, and religious tolerance. As long as whatever you're doing isn't hurting anyone, she's a fan of you, too.

Angela lives in Missouri with her husband and son. She's a member of SFWA and HWA, as well as the Four Horsemen of the Bookocalypse, her epic book critique group, where she's known as Death. When she's not swearing at the keyboard, she enjoys boating with her family at Lake of the Ozarks and reading books that raise eyebrows. You can find Angela online at **www.angelaroquet.com**

If you enjoyed this book, please leave a review. Your support and feedback are greatly appreciated!

Made in the USA
San Bernardino, CA
26 December 2019